Shades of Deception

By

Vivienne Diane Neal

Credits: Cover: Couple Illustration: © Salvatore Giannini | Dreamstime.com

Page viii: Woman at Computer Illustration: © Zig8 | Dreamstime.com

ISBN 13: 9780578031873
ISBN 10: 0578031876

This book is dedicated to my mother, my biggest supporter.

I wish to thank my loyal customers and Internet friends who have stood by me through thick and thin.

Table of Contents

Introduction

Imagine lonely people searching for love, romance or a lifetime partner on an online dating site, at a social function, through a pen pal service, on a social network or through a chance meeting and believe they have found true love and happiness only to discover that they have been deceived by heartless con artists.

Shades of Deception is a collection of ten fictional short stories centering on diverse men and women who in their speedy search for love, romance, and bliss become the targets and victims of deceit, betrayal, fraud, revenge, and scandal.

Each chapter tells a story as to how ordinary citizens who are sophisticated, successful, and financially smart fall prey to insightful predators that use love, romance, lust, and money as embellishments to destroy lives. The characters are as dynamic as the stories themselves.

Enoff is a business owner who is eager to find someone.
Passion, a pastry chef, always sees the good in people.
Marsha is the devoted and clueless wife.

Tawney, a computer developer, plans to marry a man she has only known for 24 hours.

Shaun, an ordained marriage and wedding officiant, longs to find a woman with whom to share his accomplishments.

Lea, the caterer, sets out to take her best friend's man.

Mark, the well-respected and retired math teacher will soon become the subject of scandal in his community.

Kamani, a thriving business owner thinks going the distance to find someone is the answer.

Nia, a top negotiator at a major New York brokerage firm thinks the men she keeps meeting are boring.

Jamo, a cunning college student, is about to obtain a large trust fund, which he will never get to enjoy.

The stories with their subtle adult themes and attention-grabbing plots and twists will have you turning the pages quickly to see how each character handles the bad hand dealt to them. Even though the tales are heartbreaking, the author always finds a way to add some humor to her anecdotes.

Shades of Deception

The Woman Behind The Red Curtains

People in the neighborhood were fascinated with the house on the corner, which had been unoccupied for three years. The property, with its strange past and lingering questions, had neighbors speculating as to what really happened to the couple who once lived there.

Rumor had it that Mr. and Mrs. Awa were celebrating their twenty-fifth wedding anniversary on a hot summer night. One hundred guests attended the gala, and one of the invitees was an alluring young woman. Her stunning features captivated most of the men at the party, and Mr. Awa had fallen for the enticement.

She was twenty-three; he was fifty. They started to talk, and before anyone knew it, the two snuck off to the basement and went at it like a heifer and a bull in heated passion. She had such a grip on him that the lovemaking lasted for almost two hours.

He never experienced this type of fulfillment not even with his wife, who never missed him, because she was busy attending to their guests. Being in a state of erotic bliss, he was ready to leave his spouse and live merrily ever after with the young female. Almost losing track of time, the husband rushed back to his wife and company.

Ten minutes later, the young woman followed like a silkworm coming out of her cocoon. When the party was over, the husband announced to his wife that he no longer loved her, wanted a divorce and was gone the next day.

One week later, his wife vanished. It was a mystery as to where the couple went. Many surmised that the wife might have done away with her husband, or he might have run off with his young lover. Since the couple only lived in the house for five years and kept to themselves, neighbors never got to know them. The duo would never speak to anyone and would spend weekends at Martha's Vineyard, where most of their friends lived.

The Awas were a strange match in heaven to say the least. People would refer to them as the *creepy crawler twosome*, because they would sneak out of their house to avoid running into the neighbors.

The one hundred year old Victorian style single-family house was located in Central Brooklyn, New York, a thriving village made up of professionals, artists, retirees and business owners.

Built in 1901, the 4,090 square feet three-story property had 9 furnished bedrooms, 2.5 baths, 2 total full baths, 1 total half bath and a finished basement. There were carpet, marble and linoleum floors, a spacious kitchen with a refrigerator and stove, an open dining area and an airy living room where an imported crystal chandelier hanged.

What made the home even more distinctive were its hardwood floors, decorative stairs, multi-colored walls, patterned ceilings and its steep roofing. Throughout the house were Victorian and modern furnishings, African and

Native-American paintings and exquisitely handcrafted treasures from every corner of the world.

It was never quite clear who owned the house. The neighbors assumed the couple was the rightful title-holders, but when they disappeared, several people showed an interest in buying the property, but when individuals did a title search, there were too many roadblocks. Therefore, interested parties never proceeded with the purchase.

In 2003, the house was valued at five hundred thousand dollars. Three years later, the asking price would probably be close to seven hundred thousand dollars. Nevertheless, as time went by, folks lost interest in the house and the odd couple, but soon that would all change.

A storm was about to pass through, and if the community was lacking in new chitchat, they were about to be hit with the biggest scandal that would make a soap opera look like child's play.

It was now 2006, and spring was in full swing. Flowers were blooming, and trees were thriving. High school seniors were preparing for their final exams, prom night and graduation. Couples were looking forward to their impending June weddings. The community was scheduling events for the coming months. There were planned street festivals, concerts and block parties.

People were going about their daily lives. No one noticed that someone had moved into the old Victorian house. What captured their attention were the red curtains in all the windows. *At last, someone bought the house,* many thought.

Most neighbors were surprised, because they had no idea the house was back on the market. Even the block association was clueless. Yet, everyone was delighted that the property was no longer vacant, which could have been an inducement for squatters.

It was Sunday morning, and people were going about their business or to their houses of worship. Suddenly, a limousine pulled up in front of the Victorian home. A stunning and tall woman, sporting designer sunglasses, stepped out of the limo.

She was carrying a posh black leather handbag and wearing a green silk scarf around her head, a tight-fitting burgundy dress and red high heel shoes. To say she was not fashionable would have been false. She definitely turned heads.

Because the house was on the main highway, cars were slowing down to steal a look at her. Men were gawking and drooling like roosters watching over the hen house, and women were downright appalled. Her dress was so short that everyone saw what she had for breakfast, lunch and dinner. If she were a camera, she would have snapped everyone's picture. The limo driver escorted her to the door and left. She smiled and entered the house.

The women in the community were already showing their distain for her. However, it did not matter, because she was without a doubt in harmony with the male species, so much so, that one of them would end up losing the shirt off his back.

The talk started to travel about the new woman on the block. Many would pass the house and see her behind the red curtains. Neighbors started to wonder what her game was. She had lived in the house for almost three months, and no one saw her leave the premises.

At night, prying eyes would see her nude silhouette behind the shear curtains. The men found her to be a gulp of fresh air, but the women saw her as a conniving harlot on the prowl. Many wondered if she was single or married.

Because she appeared to be in her early twenties, some started to question where she got the money to afford such an expensive home. People never saw her go to work. A few guessed she operated a home-based business, but others thought she was a kept woman.

Since many never really got a good look at her face, they all wanted to know, "What did she really look like? Who was this woman? Where did she come from, and what was her name?" The answers to those questions would come sooner than later.

While neighbors were whispering about the strange woman behind the red curtains, one of the male members of the block association decided to reach out and welcome her to the neighborhood. His name was Enoff. He was forty years old, never married and moved into the area two years ago.

His house was around the corner from hers. He owned a company that renovated and restored historic homes. The business was grossing over one million dollars a year.

Five years ago, he met a woman on an Internet dating site. Two months later, he asked her to marry him, but on the day of the wedding, she was a no-show. It turned out that she was never legally divorced and decided to reconcile with her then unemployed husband, who won the two million dollar jackpot at a casino in Atlantic City.

For Enoff, it was the ultimate humiliation. He made a promise to get to know a woman first before jumping the gun and becoming romantically involved.

His father once said, "When you become rich, there will be sharks coming out of the water to get their teeth into your money."

Enoff was lucky, because on the day of the wedding, his business was losing money. Two years later, the company became profitable, because there was a growing trend in buying and restoring old homes.

His father started the home restoration business over forty years ago. When Enoff was three years old, his parents divorced. Twelve years later, his mother remarried and relocated to North Carolina. Enoff decided to come live with his father and learned firsthand how to refurbish and repair period homes.

Enoff studied at a well-known institute and received his Master's Degree in Urban and Interior Design. After his father died, Enoff took over the company. A year after he moved into the community, he joined the block association and was responsible for bringing back over twenty-five homes to their original style and was hoping to make the Victorian house his next project.

You could say Enoff was an average looking man. He was communicative, personable and lonely. He had a few female friends, but they came without benefits. His business was very demanding, which left him very little time for dating or developing a serious romantic relationship, but he was still eager to find someone.

Although he frequently attended church, meeting the right woman was a challenge. Most of the females he encountered were calculating or looking to see how much money and material goods they could get from a man.

A few of his male employees would always complain about American women and had chosen to marry women from abroad, because they had strong family values. A man's looks, age or income was never important. Instead, these women wanted very much to be good wives, homemakers and mothers. The men always came first in their relationships.

This is not to say that Enoff wanted a meek mate, but he certainly did not want a money-hungry dominatrix in his life. He thought, maybe going outside the box could be the answer and considered going in that direction if all else failed.

It was Saturday, and Enoff went to meet with the new owner of the Victorian house. He rang the doorbell, but there was no answer. As he started to leave, the door opened and a voice said, "Hello."

When he turned around, a bee could have stung him, and he would have pleaded with the insect to nip him again. Her smile and beauty were so irresistible that he became aroused.

Breaking out in a cold sweat, he said, "Good afternoon. My name is Enoff. I am a member of the block association and wanted to welcome you to the neighborhood."

"Thank you, my name is Precious. It is a pleasure to meet you," said the woman, who invited him into her parlor.

"Enoff, please make yourself at home. Being so busy, I have not had the time to meet my neighbors but plan to have an open house soon."

She gave him a tour of the house, which was structurally sound and only needed a few minor repairs. One could say the place was well maintained but by whom? He could not remember seeing anyone going in or out of the house for two years. It was as though the property took care of itself. He definitely saw the house as an excuse to see her again and made a bid to work on its interior.

She accepted his offer with delight.

While Precious and Enoff were talking, he heard a French accent in her voice and asked if she was born in France. With crocodile tears streaming down her face, she started to talk about her long and painful journey to America.

"I was born in The Republic of Seychelles in 1980, was abandoned by my parents and grew up in an orphanage. At age eighteen, I left the institution and made my living selling costume jewelry but was barely getting by. One day, a man came to my booth and purchased all of my ornaments. It was love at first sight, and six months later, we were married. My ordeal began soon after my husband of one year started to cheat and then left me for another woman. He was a very wealthy man but was able to hide his assets in an offshore account. I ended up penniless, left everything behind and decided to come to America. Before I got married, I corresponded with an American man whom I met on-line. In his e-mails, he would always invite me to visit him. After getting married and out of respect for my husband, I ceased communicating with my friend. However, all of that changed when my spouse betrayed me. I decided to contact my pal to explain my dilemma. He invited me to come to the United States, sponsored and moved me into a studio apartment. That was three years ago. I then found a lawyer who specialized in divorce and international law. After two years of fighting for what was rightfully mine, my attorney won me a five million dollar divorce settlement; then, I heard about this house, which came with many problems and had him check into it. Even though there were some snags with the deed, I was able to buy this house. It took almost a year to straighten out the mess. It has been an agonizing journey for me, but it all ended well. My next step is to settle into my new home."

After listening to her story, one could say this woman deserved a standing ovation for her Oscar winning performance, because Enoff wanted to take her into his arms and make passionate love to her. She hooked and pulled him like a rod drawing in a defenseless fish. To him, she was the Phoenix who rose from the ashes.

This woman was going to be his wife. It was a self-fulfilling forecast, because he was thinking about going abroad to find a mate, but Precious came into his life naturally. He saw similarities between them. They both fell in love too quickly and were victims of deceitfulness. Unfortunately for him, history was about to repeat itself.

For the next several weeks, Enoff was in and out of Precious's home. He was doing minor repairs in the living room and dining area. There were times when he could not concentrate on his work. When he was alone, she was like a fierce asp and would tease and turn him on by wearing shear dresses or walking around the house topless. When there were workers with him, she was all business and *Miss Prim and Proper*. However, one warm summer evening that all changed.

While Enoff was getting ready to leave, Precious approached him in the nude, carrying a tray of refreshments. No man with a sound mind would have walked away from that sight. He stood there as if he did not know what to do next. She put the tray down, undressed him and steered him like a pro, showing a wet behind the ears man how to get it on.

They ran around the house, slid down the banisters, played hide-and-go-seek, catch me if you can, ended up in bed and made non-stop love. He could not get enough of her. When he pleaded for more, she accommodated him with her erotic force. In many ways, they balanced each other. She was yin, and he was yang. She now had him under her control and was ready to put her diabolical plan into action.

During the summer months, Enoff and Precious were having romantic trysts every other night. He could not remember being so happy and knew she was the one. He had it all worked out. He had finished the repairs in her house and had two more to restore. After completing those projects, he would take some time off from the business, take her on an extended vacation and believed Paris was the ideal place to propose.

One night, while she was sleeping, he measured her finger. The next day, he went to a high-end jeweler and ordered a blue sapphire gem set in a platinum band with four encircled diamonds. The cost was fifty thousand dollars. In one week, the ring would be ready.

After leaving the jeweler, Enoff went straight home. In his mailbox was a delivery notice for a registered letter. The next day, he went to the post office to pick up the mail, which was from a company located in London. When Enoff got home, he opened the envelope, removed the letter and started to read:

Dear Mr. Enoff:

My name is Len Trick, Barrister for Corporate Fiduciary Ltd. My client was a successful and an accomplished man, who made a large fortune before his sudden death. Since then, I have made several inquiries through your U.S.A. Embassy to locate any of my client's extended relatives, but this exercise has proven ineffective. After several unsuccessful attempts, I decided to trace his lineage on the Internet and came across your name.

To my greatest astonishment, I discovered that you bear the same surname as my late client who was born in the U.S.A. and immigrated to the UK in 1946. Convinced that my late client is a relative of yours, I decided to contact you with these facts before me.

My late client was an influential and a wealthy businessperson in the oil sector and lived in London for most of his life. He left behind a deposit of fifteen million pounds in his account at a commercial bank in London. After the death of my client, his bankers contacted me, and as his attorney, I had to find his next of kin to inherit his funds.

The board of directors of his bank adopted a resolution to provide his next of kin the payment of this money within thirty working days or forfeit the funds to the bank as abandoned property. The bankers had planned to invoke the abandoned property decree of 1996 to confiscate the funds after the expiration period given to me.

By virtue of my closeness to the deceased, I am very much aware of my client's financial standing and the bank account he managed. I feel it would be legally proper to present you as the next of kin of my deceased client, so that you can receive the funds left in his bank account.

Therefore, I seek your consent to present you as the next of kin to the deceased since you bear the same surname and birthplace. As I mentioned, the proceeds of his bank account are worth fifteen million pounds. I shall assemble all the necessary legal documents that will back up the claim.

All we require is your honest cooperation to enable us to see this deal completed. I guarantee that all claims are legitimate and will protect you from any breach of law.

Please respond by e-mail or fax.

We appreciate your immediate attention to this matter.

Mr. Len Trick, Barrister
Corporate Fiduciary Ltd.
E-mail: xyz@abc.com
Fax: +00 000 0000

After reading that letter, Enoff did not know whether to jump for joy or become a skeptic. It sounded almost too good to be true. He never heard his parents talk about any family member leaving the U.S.A. to live in the UK. He decided to call his mother and asked if she knew of any relatives living there. She mentioned that his father had a half-brother who shared the same father but had no idea where he was or if he was still alive.

The brothers met in the early 1940s but did not keep in touch. That was over sixty years ago, but she did have a photo of the two posing together and would send it to Enoff.

Meanwhile, Precious was getting ready to eat dinner. Suddenly, the doorbell rang. It was Enoff. He talked about the letter he received and gave it to her to read. If anyone could help, she would be the one.

After reading the letter, she said, "Enoff, this is great news. You never told me you had a wealthy relative living in London, you naughty boy."

They both started to laugh. She immediately offered to help him and would contact her attorney first thing in the morning. She invited Enoff to stay for dinner. After finishing their meal, the two got undressed and made blazing love for the rest of the night.

The next morning, Precious called her attorney and made an appointment for the two to meet at her home, later that day. Enoff had some work to do, left and would return in the afternoon. She quickly called the lawyer back and went over the roles they would each perform.

Enoff had finished his work on one of the houses early. When he got home, the photo of his father and uncle had arrived by special delivery. He took a quick shower and went to meet with the lawyer, who introduced himself as Mr. Chaba. He was responsible for getting the divorce settlement and assisting Precious in obtaining the house.

The attorney asked to read the letter and said he would take the case. Enoff had given him the photo his mother had sent.

"If this deceased man is a relative, this photo will be compared to his passport photo and any other pictures in Mr. Trick's possession," the lawyer said. Before he got started, he asked for a twenty-five hundred dollar retainer.

Enoff wrote a check and handed it to the attorney, who said, "I will contact Mr. Trick, send him the photo for authentication and get back to you shortly."

At the end of the week, Mr. Chaba called with great news. It turned out that the deceased man was Enoff's uncle, and since he was next in line to receive the inheritance, he would get all the money minus fees for taxes and other expenses. The lawyer gave him all the documents proving the claim, which included his uncle's birth certificate, social security number, immigration papers, passport and other pertinent credentials.

Enoff's uncle was born in the Bronx and left the United States when he was twenty-six years old. He worked his way up in the oil fields in Nigeria, invested his money in oil and natural gas and by age seventy-five was an oil baron. He never married nor had children.

The next step would be for Enoff to sign an affidavit and provide proof of kinship. That would be easy, because Mr. Chaba and Precious would be his witnesses. The lawyer drew up a sworn statement, declaring Enoff as the only living relative and successor to his uncle's inheritance and sent all of the papers to Mr. Trick.

A week later, Mr. Trick sent a letter to Mr. Chaba and a copy to Enoff, thanking them for the official declaration. Enoff could now withdraw his money from the holding bank. To make the transfer trouble-free, the bank would arrange to send the funds in US dollars, which would be approximately twenty-two million dollars.

The company needed the following information: Enoff's account number and the routing number of the bank receiving the money. It would take thirty days to complete the transaction.

As Enoff was getting ready to leave his house to go see Precious, the phone rang. It was the jeweler letting him know the ring was ready. He decided to go straight to the shop. When he saw the ring, Enoff said, "What an elegant and eye-catching treasure."

"You have excellent taste, and the woman receiving this ring will be the talk of the town," the jeweler commented.

"I was planning to wait until we went on our trip to ask her to marry me, but I am not going to put it off any longer and will ask for her hand in marriage today," Enoff replied.

"Good idea and thank you again for giving us the opportunity to serve you. Best wishes to you and your fiancée," said the jeweler.

Enoff hurried out of the store and went to see Precious. She was at the window and went to the door to greet him. "In thirty days, I will be a more affluent man and will share my wealth with you," he said.

He showed her the letter from Mr. Trick. She read it and celebrated along with him. They got undressed and made love for almost three hours. When they stopped, Enoff pulled out the ring and proposed to her. After seeing that ring, she leaped out of the bed like a jubilant cricket, ran around the room and started to do the hula dance. He got up and joined her in the ritual.

One did not have to go far to get free of charge entertainment. Precious and Enoff fulfilled that need. It was getting dark. People were on their way home from work and noticed the naked couple, behind the red curtains, boogieing to loud music, but they could not determine the identity of the man.

The two were dancing up a storm. It was as though they were in an erotic trance. She was too hot to stop, and he was in a state of intense ecstasy. Folks were still dying to know who the man was and if he was her lover or worse, someone else's husband. Every woman watching could account for her man.

Surely, she would not be bold enough to flaunt with a married man from the neighborhood, some thought.

Soon, a few of the onlookers were starting to become critical of Precious and her disgraceful conduct, but they were still watching like self-righteous overseers looking at an adult film for hours and then complaining how obscene the movie was.

Of course, most of the men found the fussing and judging to be quite humorous, because some of these same objectors had skeletons in their closets.

It was around three in the morning when Precious and Enoff ended their torrid rendezvous. Of course, she accepted his proposal and wanted to have a fall wedding. He wanted to marry her in Paris, the city of love. She thought that was a splendid idea.

He considered selling the company, retiring and traveling the world with the love of his life. With the money he was getting from his late uncle's estate, the two could live like the rich and famous. All of these dreams were racing through his head.

While Enoff was home and planning the trip to Paris, the phone rang. It was Precious informing him she had a problem with termites. Pest management was coming the following day to fumigate the house. She asked if she could stay with him until it was okay for her to return home.

"Of course, you are my fiancée, and my house is yours. By the way, I was just about to call you. I will be going upstate to finish restoring a house, will stop by in the morning and drop my house keys in your mailbox. There is plenty of food in the refrigerator. I will be home in two days."

The next day, Enoff was up at three in the morning and left the keys but had no idea Precious was dressed and ready to leave. She watched him as he drove off and waited one hour before going to his house.

It was still dark when Precious left her house. Not a soul was on the street. She scurried off to Enoff's residence, looked around to make certain no one saw her and entered his house. She found his office and went on his personal computer. However, she did not know his password and could not get into his files.

She searched through his file cabinets and found the password to his computer and the information needed to get into his on-line bank account. She took out her laptop and got into his financial records.

There was 1.5 million dollars in his business account, one hundred and fifty thousand dollars in his checking, one hundred and twenty five thousand dollars in his savings and two hundred thousand dollars in a money market account. Since he would be checking his account for the twenty-two million dollars in ten days, she had to act fast, because in one week, she would remove his money and leave the country.

It was very late when Enoff got home. Precious was up and responded to him with a wet kiss. He was delighted to see her but was tired and went straight to bed. The next day, he woke up in a horny mood and was ready for some honey. She went along with his carnal wishes, but all she could think about was all that money coming her way.

It took two days for the pesticide odor to subside. Precious decided it was time to return home and execute her final act. She made plane reservations to leave the United States in five days.

In the meantime, Enoff was planning to close the business for two months. He informed his staff that they would still be paid but decided not to sell the company. This was his legacy, and it would be like a betrayal to his father to sell the business to strangers. Moreover, he was planning to have children with Precious, and the business would be their birthright. If something were to happen to him, she and the children would be set for life. With his inheritance, he considered starting a home restoration franchise.

Enoff stopped by her house, rang the doorbell, but there was no answer. Precious was home, but she did not want to see him. It never dawned on him that she was slowly giving him the brush-off. Being on cloud nine, he was completely in the dark.

Enoff wanted to have an engagement party at his home. Since Precious did not know anyone in the community, he asked one of his female associates to help with the planning. The party would take place in one week and be a small gathering of about fifty close friends. Since he wanted it to be a surprise, he would ask her not to make any plans for that night.

When he went to visit her the next day, he said, "I have a surprise for you. Don't make any plans for next Friday evening."

"I cannot wait. Can you give me a hint?" she asked.

"No, this is why it is called a surprise," he whispered and laughed, but he had no idea that Wednesday was going to be her last day in the old Victorian house.

Two days before the engagement bash, Precious was leaving on a morning flight out of JFK International Airport. She called a cab service and was at the airport in forty-five minutes. While waiting in the terminal, she took out her laptop, logged on to Enoff's account and had all of the money from his four accounts wired into her offshore account.

She then called Enoff and told him she had decided to visit an old friend in Connecticut, would return Friday morning and asked, "What time should I be ready for the surprise?"

He told her he would pick her up at eight in the evening.

It was Friday evening, and Enoff was on top of the world. Most of the guests had arrived and were anxiously waiting to see and meet his fiancée. His mother and stepfather attended and were extremely excited that their son had finally met a fine woman. Some of the guests were members of the block association, his employees, old friends and business associates.

The catered affair, with plenty of champagne on ice, was a showstopper. He went all out for Precious and spared no expense.

It was now getting close to eight. Before leaving, Enoff dimmed the lights and requested that everyone yell "Surprise" when he and his fiancée entered the house.

When Enoff reached the Victorian house, he noticed how dark the place was. It was eerie, because the spotlight over the entrance door was always on. At first, he thought Precious did not get back from her visit. He rang the doorbell but got no answer. He called her on his cell phone, but her number was not in service. He started to get nervous and surmised that something terrible had happened to her.

He then called her lawyer, but his phone was not in service either. *What is going on here?* he asked.

As he started to leave, a woman approached him and asked, "Excuse me sir, do you live in this house?"

"No, my fiancée does, but she is not home at the moment."

The woman then went on to explain, "I met the previous owners, Mr. and Mrs. Awa, three years ago. I did not know them that well. They hired me to take photos and videotape their twenty-fifth wedding anniversary. However, here is where the story gets bizarre. The couple disappeared. Up to this date, no one knows where they went, and not a soul has come to claim their photo album and DVD, and I have been holding them ever since. Lucky for me, I got paid in full."

"That is quite a story. I have only lived in the neighborhood for two years but have heard people talk about the couple and the house, which was empty for three years," Enoff said.

The photographer then said, "I am running late and on my way to a party."

"What a coincidence, I am having a surprise engagement party for my fiancée."

"Are you Enoff?" the woman asked.

"Yes," he said.

"Your friend hired me for the evening," said the woman.

By now, Enoff knew Precious was not going to be at the engagement party. On his way back home, he had to come up with a plausible story to tell the photographer, his parents and guests.

When Enoff got home, thinking that the woman with him was his fiancée, everyone hollered, "Surprise!" He told them he had gotten a call from his fiancée; her girlfriend had a medical emergency. She did not want to leave until her friend was okay. The photographer and guests were disappointed but understood.

He told them to stay and not let the food go to waste and said, "Enjoy! We will plan another party, but this time, we will be celebrating our wedding."

Everyone applauded and started to eat. Even though Precious was not there, the photographer still took pictures and invited Enoff to her studio to look over her work in case he and his fiancée wanted to hire her for their wedding. The get-together ended around two in the morning.

It was now Monday. After seeing his parents off at the bus terminal, Enoff went straight to the studio to look at the pictures the photographer had taken at his party. In addition to showing him the proofs, she thought showing the Awas' wedding album and video would be nice since his fiancée was living in the house, which the couple once owned, and it would be the ideal place to hold their big event.

While looking through the album, he almost had a panic attack. There was a picture of his fiancée posing with an older man, whom Enoff did not know. When he inquired about the couple in the photo, the photographer did recognize the woman but did not know her name and identified the man as Mr. Awa.

Enoff thanked the photographer, took his proofs and left. He did not know what to think. Who was this Precious? Why did she not tell him that she knew the previous occupants? He started to wonder if Mr. Awa was her Internet friend, and if so, why did she keep it a secret? There were so many questions but no answers.

So preoccupied with the whereabouts of Precious, Enoff forgot about his inheritance but figured the twenty-two million dollars was already in his bank account. It did not matter if she was gone. He accepted the fact that he would never see her again. The most she got from him was a ring, which cost five figures, and fate was on his side. She could have ended up with all of his money, he concluded.

He started to wonder about her house and if the property was up for sale, again. While he was thinking about his next move, the phone rang. One of his suppliers complained that the bank returned Enoff's check because of insufficient funds. Enoff found this to be puzzling. There was enough money to cover numerous checks. He told the caller there must have been a glitch in the system and would get back to him shortly.

Enoff went on-line to check his bank account, and what he saw would have made an elephant go bananas. There was no twenty-million dollars, and all four accounts had a zero balance.

He immediately took his documents and the other papers that Mr. Chaba and Mr. Trick had sent to him and hurried to the bank; he was like a frantic man swimming after a speeding boat. To say the least, he was terrified.

When he approached the bank manager, Enoff was like a raging bull, accusing the bank of making a grave error, stealing all of his money and diverting twenty-two million dollars to heaven knows where.

The manager, with a look of concern on his face, tried to comfort Enoff. The last impression the manager wanted to project was that the institution was incompetent or crooked.

Banking customers stood there in total disbelief. Enoff was acting like a maniac. When the manager went into the computer, it showed an account outside of the United States received the money, and none of his accounts received twenty-two million dollars.

Enoff insisted that was impossible. He never performed such a task, because he had no accounts outside of the United States, and the twenty-two million dollars was an inheritance that came from a holding bank in London. He continued to be argumentative and overexcited.

The manager insisted that if he did not move the money, then who did and asked, "Did you give your personal identification number and password to anyone?"

"No!" Enoff replied in a furious tone.

Soon, the Vice President of the bank got involved. After Enoff handed all of the documents to the VP and manager, showing that the bank in London was to wire twenty-two million dollars into his account, both executives stared at each other.

They guessed that Enoff was duped big time and went on to explain he was the victim of one of the oldest con games, and many people lose all of their savings from this type of sham.

Enoff broke down, sobbed hysterically and finally got it. Precious and her cronies deceived him in such a horrific manner and took his money. He slowly got up from the chair and without saying a word, walked out of the bank and disappeared into the crowded street. No one has seen or heard from him since.

In just a matter of seconds, the gossip took on a life of its own. Just from that scene in the bank, people started to put together their own conjectures as to what really happened to flat broke Enoff.

None of the neighbors knew he was romantically involved with the woman behind the red curtains. That tidbit came out later when the clerk at the bank saw the fake documents with Precious's signature and address and immediately knew that was the old Victorian house. This is how the story got back to his neighbors.

Many would see him go in and out of her house, but they thought it was work related. The snoopy neighbors who saw her performing with an unfamiliar person behind the red curtains would have never guessed it was Enoff. He came over as such a shy and conservative person, but looks can sure be deceptive, many concluded.

When folks found out about the phony inheritance letter from London, many started to ask, "How could a smart and successful businessman fall for such a sting?"

Then, it came out that Precious never owned the Victorian house. Somehow, she and her fake lawyer manipulated the Awas into transferring the title to her, but the Awas were never the original title-holders. It was never quite clear who actually owned the house.

With the deed in shambles, people were asking, "How was Precious able to buy and move into that house?" As it turns out, she was a squatter and used the house as a front to put together her perverted scheme.

A few individuals believed she used her sexual expertise to get the better of men. It happened three years ago at the anniversary party. She was the one in the basement with Mr. Awa, and most folks believed he ran off with her, but right from the start, he was a doomed man. As to what happened to Mrs. Awa remains a mystery.

Worming her way back into town, Precious took over that house. Since no one in the neighborhood knew or recognized her, she was able to play the role of a victim with her lies, and in no time, her tentacles apprehended another poor soul, that unfortunate soul being Enoff.

Enoff's staff was completely in the dark about him and Precious. He never told anyone that the woman who lived in the Victorian house was his fiancée. Those who were with him from the start could not believe that another woman hoodwinked him, again. They thought he had learned his lesson from that first money ravenous woman.

The company was now in chaos. The employees were in limbo, and no one knew where Enoff was. Not even his mother and stepfather knew the whereabouts of their son. They reported him missing but heard nothing from the police. It was apparent he was never coming back, and eventually, the business collapsed.

Many concluded Enoff lost his mind and became a transient. The gossip went on for months and was the lead topic at every hair salon, barbershop and social event.

Tales would surface that he was collecting bottles, cans and newspapers. There was even talk that he had joined the circus. People had a tendency to stretch the truth or downright lie to outshine other gossipers.

A year had gone by, and it was now winter. Most people were hibernating due to the bitter cold and continuous bouts of heavy snow. Enoff's house went into foreclosure, and the Victorian house was still empty. The red curtains were still hanging in the windows; some individuals would still look to see if there was any activity going on in that house.

The only people who missed Precious were the men. Her antics, which they would never forget, brought life and excitement to their repetitive lives.

The local newspapers would write stories on various people and events. There was a column in one of the society papers called *What Ever Happened To...?* Occasionally, editorials would cover the whereabouts of Enoff, Precious, the Awas and Mr. Chaba. Little did anyone know that one of these individuals was living the good life in Europe.

With her red curtains dangling in the windows, Precious was now living in a villa on the Island of Capri. She was seeing a married man whom she met on an Internet dating site. He was the C.E.O. of an international trading company, traveled eight months out of the year and would spend a lot of his free time with her.

When it came to buying jewelry, he outdid Enoff and purchased a one hundred fifty thousand dollar Brazilian emerald necklace for her. It is safe to say, this man will end up losing more than the shirt off his back if he has not already.

As to what happened to the rest of the players: Mr. Chaba, a.k.a. Mr. Trick, disappeared, and Enoff and the Awas were still missing.♦

<u>Serving Time</u>

Passion always saw the good in people. Even if individuals were bad to the bone, she would look beyond their misdeeds. Raised in a household where the focus was more on spirituality, she would always hear her parents say, "There is good and bad in everyone. In some cases, the good never developed, so the bad took over that person's life. One must always look deep into an individual's heart and try to bring out that good."

Therefore, when she started to correspond with an inmate and then fell in love with him, she believed she was practicing what her parents were advocating.

However, she was about to be drawn into a network of lies, deceit and fraud, and after his release from prison, disturbing events would leave her asking, "Was he a good for nothing or the devil's spawn?"

Ever since she could remember, Passion's dream was to be a missionary. She wanted to nurture and save souls. Her caring, listening and communicating skills would have made her the ideal celebrant. She considered joining the Peace Corps but decided to stay close to home, because in her community, there were plenty of folks who needed divine intervention.

Every weekend, she would lecture to the heathens and lost souls. Yet, she possessed another great gift: Baking. When it came to her pies, cakes, tarts and cookies, she was an amazing artisan. For over twenty years, she worked as a pastry chef at the popular Gourmet Treats in Upper Manhattan, New York.

People would come from the other boroughs just to buy and taste her mouthwatering desserts. The business was doing so well that the owners decided to open a second Gourmet Treats in Carson City, Nevada, and they wanted Passion to manage the new shop; she would receive a forty percent share of the net profits.

After thinking about and discussing it with her parents, who encouraged her to go for it, she accepted the challenge.

In six months, she would be working in a city whose economic force was tourism. With visitors drawn to the casinos and other sites of interests, this shop was going to be a success if she had anything to do with it.

Since Passion had accumulated a massive amount of money and planned to purchase a home in New York City, she would use those funds to buy her first home in Carson City. She started to scout around for homes on the Internet and came across a real estate agency, which had a list of properties not too far from the new shop. After looking over numerous videos, she found a house within her price range.

Built in 2002, the single-family residence, with three bedrooms and two baths, was located approximately a quarter of a mile from the bakery. The 2,081 square feet brick home sat on five acres of land, offering complete privacy and a superlative view.

Many upgrades included carpet floors, vinyl tiles, granite counters, a top-of-the-line gas range, built-in microwave oven, stainless steel refrigerator, a laundry room, cable TV, central air conditioning, natural gas, forced air heating system, high ceilings with ceiling fans, an enclosed patio and a finished three-car garage.

The asking price was two hundred and ninety-five thousand dollars. The price was a steal, because a house like this in New York City would cost over seven figures excluding the acres of land. Because she was paying cash for the property, her bid was two hundred and eighty-five thousand dollars. The offer was accepted, and the agent would handle the deal and look after the place until Passion was ready to move in.

It would be another four months before Passion left for Nevada. She did not intend to take any of her old household belongings and decided to surf the Internet for new furnishings and accessories.

While on-line, Passion received an e-mail from a prison pen pal service called Serving Time Pen Pals Club or STPPC. The organization had been in existence for over thirty years, had thousands of members and published a monthly magazine, which listed personal profiles, photos and direct contact information of lonely male inmates, all searching for friendship, love, romance and marriage. Only non-violent inmates in minimum-security facilities could join and submit ads. Each issue had over five hundred listings.

According to some of the testimonials, many members had gotten married, and some had turned their lives around, because someone had taken the time to care by writing that first letter. An annual subscription to STPPC was thirty-five dollars. Passion immediately placed an order and could not wait to receive her first copy.

Everyone deserved a second chance, and she was going to employ what she believed in, bringing compassion and spirituality to the gone astray. Moreover, if she found love and romance, then her reaching out would not have been in vain.

Two weeks later, the first issue arrived. The layout of the publication was attractive. As she started to read the personal ads, one particular profile and photo piqued her interest:

My name is Dough, and I am an inmate at a federal correctional facility in Florida. I am a 42-year-old divorced male and wish to correspond with a single female who is open-minded, kind, considerate and independent for friendship and possibly more. I am fun loving and enjoy baking, cooking, reading and writing. Meeting new people is one of my goals, but my current situation limits my traveling. My release date is set for December 31. I will promptly answer all letters. So, please write soon.

When Passion read that ad, he held her interest. The fact that he enjoyed baking was inspiring, but his photo was downright eye-catching. His piercing brown eyes were inviting and looking straight into her heart and soul. She immediately contacted him, and for the next several weeks, they were writing each other as pen pals do.

Dough was very open about himself. Fifteen years ago, he and a college friend started a consulting firm, which helped small and medium-size businesses become more efficient and profitable. The two created great marketing and advertising ideas that generated continuous earnings for their clients.

However, his partner had embezzled over one million dollars, committed mail fraud, vanished and left Dough holding the bag. Employees of the company lost all of their retirement savings, and the corporation folded. He ended up serving five years for a crime he had no knowledge of or committed. He lost his home; his wife divorced him, and his family and so-called friends abandoned him. Trying to prove his innocence to no avail, he became disillusioned. Passion's letter was the first piece of communication he had received since serving time. In one of his letters, he wrote:

Most inmates doing time never get to have pen pals or visits from relatives or friends. They are always hoping that someone will give them a chance to form a lasting friendship by taking the time to write a letter.

In addition, an inmate's contact with the outside world is a positive step, especially if that connection is with someone who is ready to encourage that individual to evaluate his past and bring about the changes necessary for him to lead a fruitful life when released from prison.

The first letter I received from you brought me so much happiness and restored my faith in humanity.

Now, I am ready to face whatever life throws my way with you by my side.

Overwhelmed by his sincerity, Passion started to fall for this man and knew what she had to do next, help restore his sense of worth.

The two were now corresponding by e-mail. Passion mentioned her new role as manager of a gourmet bakery in Carson City and wanted Dough to work with her. Since his areas of expertise were marketing and advertising and with his love for baking, he would be a perfect fit for the company. He was interested in her proposition but questioned how was he going to get to Nevada, and where was he going to stay since he had very little money. To ease his mind, she wrote:

I just purchased a home with plenty of space, and you will have your own room and complete privacy; I will send you a plane ticket and enough money to get started until you get back on your feet. As manager of the store, I will split my profits with you.

No man in his right mind would have turned down an offer like that. Keyed up, he accepted her invitation and made a promise to be a righteous man.

The owners were preparing Passion for the takeover of the new shop, which would open in two months. She informed them that she knew a business consultant who could be her associate store manager and assistant pastry chef, and he was planning to relocate to Carson City at the end of the year. Of course, she never mentioned he was an inmate who was about to be released soon.

Whether the owners would have approved of an ex-con working at their business never came up during work-related discussions.

Not everyone shared her philosophy of forgiving or granting people a second chance. Some of her co-workers and close friends thought she was too trusting and giving, especially when it came to men. She always had that eager to please syndrome, which in the end would cause her demise.

In two weeks, Dough would be a free man and on his way to Carson City. Passion instructed the real estate agent to provide a house key for him upon his arrival. It would be another month before she would join him.

When Dough got to the house, the real estate agent was there and handed him the key. He thanked the agent and let himself in. To say he was not impressed with the house would have been a fib. He could not fathom being in such an exquisite setting. Nicely outfitted with chic furnishings and elegant accessories, it was a scenic place.

After spending five years in a dormitory style housing that consisted of numerous cots in a large room, this is a five star villa, he thought.

He toured the house, selected his room and was ready to execute his underhanded plan. As he was unpacking, the house phone rang. It was Passion, letting him know that in two weeks the owners were coming to Carson City to check on the shop and wanted to meet with him for an informal interview.

She reiterated, "There was no mention about you serving time."

Dough reassured her that everything was under control. They talked for about two hours. After getting off the phone, he put together an impressive résumé and listed three references. On his way from the airport, he remembered passing a copy place, which was within walking distance from the house.

The next day, he took a draft copy of his vita to the printer and had it professionally typed. Two days later, the document was ready. He then went to a men's clothing shop and purchased a couple of suits, shirts, ties, a pair of shoes and a leather attaché case. He was now ready to play the most compelling role of his life.

The owners had flown in to check on the bakery, which was going through some last minute modifications. They were anxious to meet with Dough, called and invited him for a get together at his convenience. To scrutinize the layout of the shop, he thought meeting there would be perfect and agreed to meet with them the following day.

Dough rehearsed his lines in front of the mirror and foresaw every question the owners would pose. He knew they would check his references and had that area covered; he left nothing to chance. He laid out his garments and had his résumé along with an introductory letter in an elegant dossier. Stating that this man was not on top of his game was like saying, "The dog was not a descendant of the wolf."

It was just a matter of time before he would con the owners, wreck them financially and leave Passion holding the sack.

On the day of the interview, it was a bright and sunny day. Dough woke up feeling victorious. He took a shower, got dressed and was ready to leave for his meeting. Since the shop was not too far from the house, he decided to walk, which gave him enough time to practice his script.

When he arrived at the bakery, the owners were already there. With a gleam on their faces, they introduced themselves as Cid and Betty.

Dough responded by saying, "It is a great honor to meet you; Passion has told me so much about you and your other shop in New York."

"Likewise," said the owners, who started to give him a tour of the place; he made a mental note of the shop's layout. It was spacious and well designed with earth tone colors and trendy exhibit cases. The enclosed back area was where the baking would take place. On each side was an office. The front area was indicative of a specialty gourmet shop with enhancing wooden floors.

Because the shop was on a highway, the area was a crowd-puller; the business would unquestionably make tons of money. As the three sat down, Dough talked about his business background as a consultant and came up with many thoughts as to how the shop could pull in more money.

He recommended setting up a mail order department and emphasized, "This way, you could build a customer mailing list and during special events or holidays send out flyers or brochures announcing new products and special sales. To build your in-house mailing list, you could have customers sign their name and address in a guestbook before leaving the shop. In the near future, you can have a presence on the World Wide Web and quadruple your revenues."

Dough's suggestions swept away the owners. After reading his résumé, they were even more amazed. The owners were pleased with his creative talents and professionalism. They offered him the job as Director of Marketing and Advertising, but first, they had to check his references and would get back to him shortly.

A week later, Dough heard from Cid and Betty. After checking his character references and hearing glowing accounts of how he made millions for his clients, they offered him the job as head of marketing and advertising.

After getting that good news, he made several phone calls and said to the people on the other end, "It's a done deal."

Later that evening, Dough called Passion and gave her an update. So overjoyed, she could not wait to see and work with him. Still, it was not clear if he would be her partner or an employee.

She contacted the owners and inquired about Dough's employment status. They informed her that he would be on probation for six months. If things worked out, he would have the option to become her associate partner.

In two days, Passion was due to arrive in Carson City. Dough was getting his act together and coming up with the grand scheme of all schemes.

In twelve months, someone would make an offer to Cid and Betty to buy the two shops. It would be a well thought-out plot. He knew three ex-offenders who would participate in the deception. They would pretend to be investors and handle all transactions. Two offshore bank accounts would be set up in countries that had no extradition treaties. These types of depositories were great, because they usually left no paper trail.

Passion's flight arrived on time. She called Dough from the airport to let him know she was on her way. In forty-five minutes, she was home. When she opened the door, he was standing there; they embraced and kissed each other like overzealous fleas.

What a rubenesque beauty, he thought.

What a hunk, she thought.

Dough looked as if he had just stepped out of a men's fashion magazine. He was tall, muscular and downright attractive. Completely fulfilled, she knew he was going to be her better half. It was positively love at second sight.

Passion went to her room, got undressed and took a long hot bubble bath. While she was relaxing in the tub, sensual thoughts started to seep into her head. Finally, she got out of the tub, dried off and got dressed. When she entered the dining area, dinner was waiting.

The two sat down, started to talk and were delighted to meet in person. She was thankful he got the job and talked about applying unique strategies to make the business successful and profitable.

Today was the grand opening of Gourmet Treats. The shop was selling an assortment of cakes, cookies, tarts, cupcakes, muffins, gift tins and gift baskets.

The first week's opening was an overall success with over fifty thousand dollars in sales. By the end of the month, the store made over two hundred and fifty thousand dollars. The mail order department was taking off like gangbusters. Three months later, sightseeing companies were scheduling bus tours to the shop.

The owners could not have predicted the place would become one of the most popular spots in such a short period. Word of mouth about Gourmet Treats was spreading faster than a running back carrying the ball across the opponent's goal line. People were arriving from all over, and eventually, orders were coming in from around the world.

Two additional employees were hired, and in six months, Dough became an associate partner. He and Passion were now running a booming and lucrative business.

Cid and Betty felt the shop was now sound and decided to return to New York.

It did not take long for Passion and Dough to become somewhat romantically involved. When they got home from work, the two would engage in foreplay, but he would always pull back. She found this to be quite exciting and odd at the same time but admired him for not succumbing to her lustful desires.

Most of the men she met in the past were only interested in getting it and moving on to the next conquest; she learned that a respectable man would take things at a snail's pace and get to know a woman first before rushing into bed with her. Therefore, she would have waited longer for him to come around.

In its first year, Gourmet Treats netted two million dollars, and customers could now go on-line to place orders, thanks to Dough. While at work, he called one of his cohorts to put his plan into motion. It was easy to call from his office, because it was private with no one to eavesdrop on his conversations. Whenever he made calls to his contacts, he would always use disposable cell phones.

In New York, Cid and Betty were facing a dilemma. A new owner was purchasing the building that housed their shop. The present lease was no longer enforceable. There would be a one hundred percent increase in the rent. They were already paying close to fifty thousand dollars a month.

With the new increase, rent would be over one hundred thousand dollars a month. At this point, they were ready to close that bakery and focus on the one in Carson City.

Two days later, they received a call from an investor, who along with other backers was interested in buying both Gourmet Treats.

Because of the shops' unique product line, good management and potential sales growth, the venture capitalists saw a great opportunity to expand Gourmet Treats into a global phenomenon by opening shops in various countries. They wanted to meet with the owners and make an offer that would leave the couple set for life.

Cid and Betty were quite intrigued and agreed to get together with the investors, who would be in New York at the end of the week.

Back in Carson City, Dough was making plans to move money from Gourmet Treats' account and the owners' joint account into an offshore account. He was able to hack into the couple's financial records and obtain their username, password and personal identification number.

How he was able to accomplish this was unknown. The business account had over three million and the joint account close to two million dollars.

Passion was in a world of confusion. All she thought about was Dough and wondered why he did not want to make love to her. After all, they had lived together for over a year. She saw herself as a sexy and desirable woman.

What is the problem? Perhaps he is impotent or not into me, she imagined.

On the job, he was all business. She would try to get his attention by flirting with him and wearing seductive clothing, but these tactics were ineffective.

Lastly, she came up with a line of attack that would answer her query. *Is he in love with me or not?*

The next day, Passion left work early, went home and prepared some spicy dishes, which would stimulate his sexual appetite and had Cold Duck on ice. She removed her garments, took a shower, got out and sprayed her body with a lavender scented splash. She played some soft romantic music, got into his bed and waited.

As soon as Dough arrived home, the melody and the aromatic food spellbound him. When he walked into his bedroom, Passion was naked as a jade bird and had positioned herself like a lady in waiting. He stood there with a devious grin, got undressed, and before she could open her mouth, he was going at it like a greyhound trying to break the speed record.

If she thought the lovemaking was going to last for eternity, it would never happen. In two minutes, it was over. He gave a completely new meaning to the idiom, *biff bam, thank you ma'am*. She was flabbergasted. It was the fastest undertaking she had ever encountered, and after his quick presentation, he fell asleep. She got up, went to her bedroom and started to sob.

The interested buyers and their lawyer met with Cid and Betty. The investors presented a proposal and offered them ten million dollars for both Gourmet Treats. If they wanted to, they could stay on as consultants and receive twenty percent of the net profits. The owners felt the bid was an excellent one but did not wish to stay on as advisers but placed a stipulation before selling the business: Passion and Dough would have to stay on in their current positions.

The backers agreed. Dough and Passion would manage both shops or hire someone to run the New York City one and have complete autonomy. As long as the two were meeting projected revenues, the investors would remain silent.

Since Cid was a paralegal, he read the contract, and everything seemed to be in order. He and Betty signed the agreement. In one week, they would receive a cashier's check.

That evening, Dough received a call from one of the men saying, "They took the bait."

It was early Friday morning and Dough's last day in Carson City. Passion was already awake. As she was getting ready to take a shower, Dough grabbed and kissed her; they ended up making love for almost two hours.

She was overjoyed and shouted, "I love you and want to be your wife."

"I have always loved you but did not want to rush into a serious relationship and wanted to make certain you wanted to be with me, and now I am ready to commit myself to you forever," he said.

She succumbed to his lines and was ready to be with him without end but had no clue it would be her last day with him.

They left for work, but Dough had to make a stop and pick up a gift for Passion. He would see her in a couple of hours. In her mind, he was making it official and buying her an engagement ring.

Before Dough left for the airport, he went back to Passion's house. He got on her computer, logged into Cid and Betty's personal and business accounts and moved all of the funds into an offshore account. He left the house, hailed a cab to the airport, got on his flight and landed in Mexico. He went to The Global Bank of Mexico and had over five million dollars wired into another offshore account, which was somewhere in South America.

It was already two in the afternoon, and Passion was patiently waiting for Dough to come to work. She was beginning to wonder if something had happened and called home to see if he was there, but there was no answer.

The shop was crowded with tourists, and the phones were ringing non-stop. The two other employees were at their wits end, juggling the phones, attending to mail and on-line orders and waiting on customers. There was so much chaos; a line started to form outside of the shop and around the block.

It was now six in the evening. Things had slowed down, and yet, there was still no sign of Dough. As Passion was getting ready to leave work, she thought about calling the police but believed an adult had to be missing for at least twenty-four hours before law enforcement would do anything.

She went home, hoping he would be there, but he was not. As she started to get undress, the phone rang, but it was the wrong number. When she went into his room, all of his belongings were gone. It still did not dawn on her; he had left for good.

Confused, Passion did not know what to feel. *He would never leave without saying something*, she thought. The next day, she reported him missing.

A week later, Cid and Betty received a cashier's check for ten million dollars and deposited the check into their joint account. A couple of days later, they decided to move funds from the business account into their joint account. What they were about to discover would leave them in a state of shock and disbelief. The business account had a zero balance.

When they confronted the bank manager about the error, the administrator said, "You moved your money from the business account into a foreign bank account."

Cid and Betty looked at each other as though the woman was speaking in tongues. They insisted that no such transaction occurred, that the bank made a gross blunder and to check and correct the mistake, or they would sue the institution for blatant negligence.

If they thought they had put the fear of God into the bank executive, they were about to face the most terrifying event of their lives. The ten million dollar check, which they deposited into their joint account, was bogus, and the balance was one hundred dollars.

What happened next would leave customers and the business community asking, "Who swindled whom?"

When Passion learned what had happened to Cid and Betty, she was stunned. For all purposes, the shop was out of business. She thought maybe she could continue to run the shop or perhaps purchase it, but where was she going to get that kind of money? Everything was now in disarray.

A computer technician was able to pinpoint the moving of the money from the owners' bank accounts back to Passion, because all of the transactions took place on her personal computer; it was unknown where the money went.

When confronted with this information, Cid and Betty held Passion responsible for their financial fall and pointed the finger at her for embezzling five million dollars. After all, she was the manager, and the buck stopped at her doorstep.

Passion finally got it. Dough had set her up right from the start. He was never in love with her. Now, in the same mess as she believed he was once in, her bosses were accusing her of a crime she had no knowledge of or committed.

When the scandal broke about Gourmet Treats, the media had a field day, and people in Carson City and New York were gossiping like guests at a hen party.

A few individuals believed Passion and Dough were in on the fraud. Others thought Cid and his wife Betty moved the money to an offshore account to avoid paying taxes.

It was strange that the owners would sell their business to complete strangers and not first have their lawyer investigate these so-called financiers, some reflected. The circumstances under which the deception took place were mind-boggling.

Nevertheless, Passion had an ultimatum: Either she would have to repay all of the money, or Cid and Betty would press charges against her. Since she did not have that kind of cash, she was prepared to go to prison.

After six months of probing and legal finagling, all the evidence pointed to Passion; she decided to plea no contest to fraud and received ten years' probation, and as restitution, she had to relinquish all of her personal assets and real property to Cid and Betty. They would also garnish any future income until all five million dollars was paid in full.

Because Passion had no criminal record, she got off easy. Many of her loyal customers, friends and relatives came to her defense and spoke very highly of her.

After learning Dough had once served time for misappropriation of funds, everyone guessed he and he alone was behind the offense.

Countless people thought the owners of Gourmet Treats treated Passion unjustly; they knew deep down in their hearts she would have never committed such a diabolical act; it was not in her nature. The fact that she worked for these people for over twenty years and made bundles of money for both shops meant nothing to them. They went after her as a cat would go after a mouse, without mercy.

At the end, Passion did share some of the blame for her own stupidity. By not doing a comprehensive background check on Dough, she had premeditated her own downfall.

A year had gone by, and Passion was now living in a boarding house with five other people. The environment was a complete contrast to where she had once lived. She occupied a room, had to share the bathroom and kitchen with the other tenants and worked as a pastry chef at a neighborhood restaurant in Reno.

Because Cid and Betty were garnishing half of her paycheck, she was barely getting by. The more money she made in over-time, the more money they got. It was a never-ending battle to make ends meet.

She often thought about Dough and wondered how he was able to live with himself, using her and the owners in such an atrocious manner. She later learned he was the one who embezzled the money from his own company. There was never any partner.

It was obvious to Passion that he lacked moral character and was a good for nothing villain; she thought back to those words her parents had delivered and concluded, *There was never any good in him, and no amount of heavenly intervention would have saved his soul. He was a progeny of the devil.* She also recognized a leopard never changes its spots.♦

Blindsided By Love and Desire

There was a knock at the door. Marsha had just awakened from a bad dream and could not picture who was visiting her so early in the morning.

At first, she thought it was her husband, but he would have his keys and was not due back from his trip for at least another month. She went to the door; it was the mail carrier. He handed her a certified package that required her signature. When she opened the envelope, a petition for the dissolution of marriage was enclosed.

She knew the marriage was on shaky grounds but never imagined it would end like this, in such a cold and an impersonal manner. She wondered how Ted, her husband of five years, could have ended their marriage in such a sneaky way.

The ideal wife is how Marsha saw herself, the one who always stood by her husband no matter how bad things got. She supported him financially and emotionally, helped him finance a couple of business ventures and took care of his sisters who gave an entirely new meaning to the word moochers. She had put her needs on hold to help her husband fulfill his, and for all of her sacrifices, this is how he repaid her.

But if she thought getting those divorce papers was a slap in the face, she was about to be blindsided by events that would place her into financial ruins and leave her parents, friends and neighbors saying, "We saw it coming."

Marsha met Ted at a singles' dance. She was 24; he was 28. It was definitely love at first sight on her part, but it was never quite clear if he had those same feelings.

She had just graduated from college with a Degree in Accounting. Her goal was to work in her father's firm for a couple of years and then take the New York State Licensing Exam to become a Certified Public Accountant. Those plans never materialized once she got involved with Ted.

Three months later, they eloped to Delaware and tied the knot; it would be several more months before anyone knew they were husband and wife.

Those who knew Ted were wondering how he landed such a classy woman and were starting to question Marsha's state of mind when she married him. After all, she came from a well-to-do family.

Her father had started his own advertising business five years before she was born, and her mother was the publisher and editor of a popular weekly society newspaper.

Marsha went to the finest schools that money could buy. She maintained an A average throughout high school and college and was valedictorian at her college commencement. She and her parents lived in a picturesque mansion in the Stuyvesant Heights section of Brooklyn,

New York. Marsha was a beautiful and refined young woman. She was tall, had the air of a monarch and wore designer clothes.

Being an only child, Marsha was somewhat spoiled but was never condescending to those who were less fortunate. She was a down-to-earth person, unlike her parents who were the epitome of snootiness. She and her parents traveled a great deal, which made her a well rounded and an open-minded individual.

Ted was the eldest of three children; his parents died in a car accident when he was twelve years old. He and his sisters who were ten and eight at the time were the beneficiaries of their parents' insurance policy and lived with various family members.

By the time they became teenagers, the insurance money ran out and so did their relatives, and even though the siblings were virtually raising themselves, they were forever there for each other through the good and bad times and made a promise to continue to be there for each other, no matter what.

In his junior year, Ted dropped out of high school. He did manage to get his GED, but holding down a steady job was not one of his strongest points.

His sisters were attending college, but they never completed their studies, and as far as the neighbors knew, they never held down a steady job either.

Yet, Ted did manage to obtain an apartment building that consisted of sixteen units. The property was worth two hundred and fifty thousand dollars. In a short period, the building became a source of income for the three siblings. People who knew of them were trying to figure out how these three, who appeared to be flat broke and busted, were able to pull off such a coup.

When Marsha's parents learned about the marriage, they were livid, to say the least. After all, they knew nothing about this man. In fact, they never even met him. The two were secretly seeing each other, because Marsha knew her parents would be against it. What was the rush her parents pondered?

At first, they thought their daughter was pregnant, but that was not the case. She would have walked through the flames of hell to be with him eternally. It was as though she became spellbound when she first laid eyes on him. It was ironic, because he did not have much going for him when it came to looks, grace and social status. No one would have written home about him.

Even if their lives depended on it, her girlfriends would have never given Ted a second look or the time of day. He could be loud and uncouth at times, and many saw him as an individual who lacked good manners and class.

Her parents loathed him and believed their daughter could have done so much better. She always dated upstanding and sophisticated men; they were highly educated, held prominent positions in various fields and were financially sound; they were the crème de la crème. So why would she have settled for someone like Ted?

The fact that he had property meant nothing, because based on the stories they heard, her parents started to wonder how someone who never held down a steady job or had a pot to make coffee in was able to get an apartment building worth six figures.

Nevertheless, Marsha made it clear to her parents; she was head-over-heels in love with him, and they would have to accept it, or she would be out of their lives for good.

At the end, her parents did back down, but they never accepted Ted or his sisters into the family; they just tolerated them for the benefit of their daughter. Yet, deep in their hearts, her parents and everyone else in the community knew the marriage was a disaster right from the start. Unfortunately, it would take Marsha five years to come to this realization.

Three years prior to meeting Marsha, Ted had elaborate ideas for the property he obtained, which was located in an industrial area. His first plan of action was to send out notices to all the tenants, informing them that the building was now under new ownership, and whatever agreement they had with the previous owner was no longer binding.

He then increased the rent by twenty-five percent, which was payable to Ted and Associates; the associates were his sisters. All occupants were on a month-to-month lease, and rent was due on the first of the month with a ten-day grace period. If a tenant did not pay his or her rent within ten days, he would evict that person.

Since Ted wanted three of those apartments, one for himself and two for his sisters, those renters received removal notices and had thirty days to leave.

The building was in superb condition and well maintained. The lobby had marble tiled floorings and stucco walls. The ceiling, with its beautiful handcrafted and intricate patterns, stood 12 feet high. There was a courtyard where residents could entertain or have cookouts. The finished basement was a laundry room, which had six washers and four dryers.

Ted's apartment had three large bedrooms, one full bathroom and a spacious living room with parquet floors, a large kitchen with modern appliances and an open dining area.

His sisters had their own one bedroom apartment with similar details. If either of his sisters ever required more space, he would just send kicking out letters. He had assigned his sisters to keep the books for the property, collect rents, deposit checks and pay all the bills and taxes.

After the marriage, Marsha moved out of her parents' home and into Ted's apartment; she added her own decorative touches and brought life to their dreary place.

Throughout her travels, Marsha collected paintings, artifacts and mementos, which adorned their living room and bedroom; she even converted one of the bedrooms into an art gallery. If her husband had any appreciation for her decorating abilities, he never said a word.

Amazed at her work, Ted's sisters requested that she give their apartments a face-lift, and she agreed. For the next few months, she was adding her artistic expertise to their rooms. When he saw his sisters' quarters, it got him thinking as to how he could make extra money from his wife's talents.

Since the couple did not have a proper wedding ceremony, Marsha decided to have a belated reception and celebrate their approaching one-year anniversary. She could not decide whether to have the reception in their courtyard or at a popular catering site. One of her father's associates owned an elaborate banquet hall.

Her sister-in-laws thought having the event at the hall was the grandeur way to go, but Ted made it very clear that the cash flow was limited for such an extravagant affair. The income from rents had to go back into the property for upkeep, taxes, utilities and other expenditures.

Marsha decided to foot the bill for the gathering. To avoid any type of fuss, she did not want to ask her parents for assistance and went to the bank to withdraw enough money from her trust fund to put a down payment on the dining room.

Ted showed very little interest during the planning stages of the pending affair. His wife and sisters took care of those details. It took about three months to make all of the final preparations. The function was to take place on a Saturday evening from 6:00 p.m. until midnight.

Over three hundred and fifty invitations went to family, friends and business associates; they had three weeks to respond. Nearly all of the invitees answered yes.

For the gala, Marsha had her gown made by a well-known designer, who lived a couple of blocks from her parents.

Ted's sisters were supposedly financially strapped and could not afford to have their gowns custom-made, but their sister-in-law took care of that.

Because of time constraints, Marsha took the sisters to a high-end dress shop. Of course, they each chose the most expensive gown in the shop, costing nearly one thousand dollars each. They were going to be the belles of the ball and the center of attention not their sister-in-law.

A month before the affair, Marsha took her husband to an exclusive men's shop to have his tuxedo tailor-made, which was a perfect fit. He was now ready to make his introduction to the upper crust of society.

The night of the soirée was finally here. The weather was ideal with temperatures in the mid 70s. The sky was clear; one could have seen the stars without end. Everything seemed to be going exactly as planned.

Marsha, Ted and his sisters arrived at the location early. It was a well-designed place. There would be a cocktail hour followed by a four course sit-down dinner.

The six-tiered wedding cake was a work of art, which was worthy of the blue ribbon award. The dining room was definitely the best spot for a wedding celebration and the most inviting environment a couple could ever want.

The first guests to arrive were Marsha's parents; they greeted their daughter with a big hug and gave her an envelope. However, they completely ignored her husband

and his sisters as though they were nonexistent. The waiter escorted the parents to their table.

Shortly after, more guests started to arrive, bringing praises and gifts. Everybody who was somebody attended the celebration. Those present, with the exception of Ted's sisters, were all relatives and friends of the bride and her parents. Guests talked to the couple and wished them a happy and lasting marriage.

Yet, no sooner after helping themselves to the hors d'oeuvres and cocktails and then sitting down at their tables did those well-wishers start to talk about the couple like a swarm of bees gathering nectar and pollen from flowers. It was as though the invitees had come to gossip rather than commemorate the couple's nuptial and one-year anniversary.

People were actually placing bets that the marriage would not last too much longer.

Some went so far to say, "Ted married Marsha for her huge trust fund."

Many inferred that he and his sisters got that apartment building in a fraudulent way.

A few wondered why his other relatives and friends were not present at such an important occasion and suggested his sisters were not his true siblings but his paramours.

It was no doubt an etched in your mind night accompanied by some unsubstantiated innuendos and enjoyable anecdotes.

It was now close to midnight, and people were starting to leave. Marsha thanked everyone for their presence and wished them a safe trip home.

She complimented the owner of the hall for a job well done and paid the balance owed on the function. The total cost for the event was seventy-five thousand dollars.

When the couple arrived home, they discussed how the night had gone with Marsha doing most of the talking. The gifts took up half of the apartment. Ted had gone to bed, while she prepared for a night of playful pleasures.

If Marsha really thought there was going to be a night of hot and heavy lovemaking, she was sadly in the wrong. When she walked into the bedroom, Ted was dead to the world, snoring louder than a herd of cattle charging through the prairie.

For the next couple of weeks, Marsha was busy opening gifts and sending out personal thank you notes. Sometimes, there were two of the same gifts, but her sister-in-laws were delighted to take those extra presents off her hands.

While taking a break, she remembered the envelope her parents had given her. She had placed it in her evening bag and had forgotten all about it. When she opened it, there was a deed to a house in the Bahamas.

Twenty years ago, her parents had purchased that house, which was on the island of Nassau. They titled the house in their daughter's name. Completely stunned, she called her parents and thanked them for the gift.

The house had four bedrooms and four baths. There was central air conditioning and ceiling fans in every room. The state-of-the-art kitchen had marble-tiled floors, custom cabinetry with granite countertops and all stainless steel appliances. There was a sophisticated electronic control system throughout the house, a theater room, and a single garage. The outdoor living space included a forty-inch pool and spa, a guesthouse and a private beach.

When Marsha shared the good news about the house with Ted, a light bulb went off in his head as to how he could turn her island home into a gold mine.

The couple was now approaching their second anniversary. Since they never had a honeymoon, Marsha thought spending a week in Nassau would get Ted's mind off business. He was hard at work, managing and maintaining the property, that the couple was spending less time together.

When she approached him with the suggestion, he quickly turned it down and told her, with property tax, utilities and other expenses escalating, not enough revenue was coming in to afford such a trip. Therefore, he could not leave town now. He did propose that she could go and take his sisters with her.

"They have never traveled outside of the United States, and it would be a life changing experience for them. Besides, there will be plenty of time for trips abroad in the near future when there is more money coming in from a new business venture I am planning to start."

Marsha was confused and asked, "What new business venture?"

He started to explain his plans to convert four apartments into condominiums, and if all goes well, he would do the same with the remaining units. He told her he got the idea when he saw what she had done to theirs and his sisters' apartments. He figured he could sell the decorated condominiums to people who just did not have the time to design or beautify their place.

It would be ideal for people who traveled often or did not live in their residence throughout the year. In fact, owners would have the option to sublet their space.

Ted could see the money rolling in like water flowing down a stream. Marsha thought the idea was an excellent one. He started to put together a business plan and drafted the following letter:

Dear Tenants:

Plans are in the works to convert your apartment into a condominium; you will have the option to buy into the unit and pay a monthly maintenance fee. Based on the number of rooms you have, the asking price would vary. A three-bedroom unit would sell for eight hundred and fifty thousand dollars, two bedrooms for six hundred and fifty thousand dollars and a one bedroom for four hundred and fifty thousand dollars.

You will receive additional information in the coming months.

Ted and Associates

"But a project like this will cost a lot of money," he said.

Since Ted was barely getting by on the income from rental fees, he would have to borrow the money or take out a second mortgage on the building and would need roughly three hundred thousand dollars to get the ball rolling.

"Where am I going to get that much money?" he asked his wife.

She came up with an idea and said, "I could give you the money from my trust fund. After all, what's mine is yours, and what's yours is mine."

With a big smile on his face, he accepted her offer. A week later, she went to the bank and had a cashier's check for three hundred thousand dollars made out to Ted and Associates. He and his sisters were eternally grateful; he went to his bank and deposited the check.

In the meantime, Marsha started to jot down some designing and decorating ideas for the soon-to-be condominiums and concluded this would be her calling: Starting a home decorating and designing business.

For the next two years, it appeared as though Ted was trying to get his condominium development off the ground. For reasons unknown to Marsha, the plan fell through. He gave her a long song and dance that there were too many legal hassles; half of the money went towards legal advice and the remaining to contractors, engineers, architects and draftspersons for construction, renovation and projection studies.

Due to zoning laws, the conversion could not take place. All the money was gone. It turned out to be a bad investment.

Nevertheless, his wife believed it was a wonderful plan. "Perhaps the timing was not right," she concluded.

However, her husband had another ace up his sleeve. He saw renting out stylish and elegant furnished apartments as the way to go. With her help, he would provide empty units with contemporary furniture, high-tech appliances, artwork, imported rugs, vivid walls and motif ceilings. Ted was cooking with gas, and Marsha was going along with the sales pitch.

There was a vacant one-bedroom apartment. He anticipated it would cost approximately thirty-five thousand dollars to revamp the place. Seeing this as a great investment, she went to the bank and withdrew the money from her trust fund.

In two months, the rent for the furnished apartment was two thousand dollars a month.

To say the marriage was heavenly would have been imaginary. Going into their fifth year of matrimony, Ted and Marsha were drifting apart. There was very little intimacy in the bedroom. The sisters were squandering Marsha's money and spending more time in Nassau. Ted never went to the island to see the house.

When Marsha did go to the Bahamas, she usually went alone, with the sisters or with close friends. Ted had been very distant with her. She thought there was another woman, but he never showed any signs of infidelity.

She never let on to anyone or to her parents about the impasse in their marriage, because she did not want to hear: "We told you so!" Besides, she felt things would get better, because every marriage goes through growing pains.

Marsha went back to the first night they met. Ted was so attentive and considerate. They enjoyed doing things and spending time together; three months later, they got married, but after the marriage, she slowly noticed a change in him.

Ted was more and more preoccupied with the property and coming up with moneymaking dreams that never worked. When it came to making business decisions, he would always consult with his sisters; they had more of an influence over him than Marsha did. It was as though she was just a minor player in a mismatched relationship but quickly went back to happier thoughts, because she knew the marriage was going to get better.

Ted's sisters enjoyed the island of Nassau so much that they decided to stay there permanently. How they managed to do this was anyone's speculation. Ted had no problems renting out their apartments. As soon as he placed an ad in the newspaper, several prospective renters called to inquire about the units. Within one month, both apartments were bringing in four thousand dollars per month.

It was Saturday morning when the doorbell rang. Ted had answered the door, received an important letter and read it. He had the biggest grin on his face and told Marsha he had to leave town at once to check on a parcel of land, which he was planning to purchase.

Marsha wanted to accompany him, but he asked her to remain home, because he had a surprise for her. She anticipated he was buying that land for her, because her birthday was coming soon. She smiled and helped him pack.

In three days, Ted was gone, and that was the last time she saw him. After getting those divorce papers, she theorized this was his surprise.

Since they did not accumulate large amounts of assets during their years together, the termination of the marriage was simple. There were no major possessions to divide.

Ted purchased his building before they got married, and the house Marsha received from her parents was hers. Since she had no intentions of contesting the divorce or asking for alimony, she signed the papers and returned them in the enclosed self-addressed stamped envelope. She was now legally divorced.

After remaining in the apartment for six months, Marsha started to look for another place to live. She no longer wanted to stay in Ted's apartment building and thought about moving back home with her parents but decided not to.

Not that her parents would not have welcomed her back home, quite the contrary; they would have jumped for joy to know their daughter had finally come to her senses and said adieu to that leech of a so-called husband.

Her parents would have been stunned if they knew their daughter was the one dumped. It would not be long before the truth would come out.

Marsha found a nice studio apartment in Brooklyn Heights. Since there was not much money left in her trust fund, she would rent out her island home to bring in additional income and work on expanding her business.

If Marsha thought she was finally free of Ted, she had another thought coming. There were more problems brewing. While she was packing, to move into her new place, a letter arrived from the Property Tax Assessment Department. She opened it and could not believe what was in that letter. The apartment building was in arrears for back taxes, which totaled over six hundred thousand dollars.

How could Ted have let this tax thing get out of control? What was he doing for the past eight years? The money he collected in rents should have been going towards paying the property tax.

Two months later, Marsha received a letter forwarded to her new address from the Internal Revenue Service; she and Ted owed over four hundred and fifty thousand dollars in back taxes.

Then, she discovered he and his sisters did not own the apartment building. The previous owner never intended to sell or give the property to anyone; the proprietor suffered from short-term dementia and unknowingly signed the title over to Ted.

Somehow, Ted and his sisters were able to manipulate the man into thinking Ted was his long-lost son. Since the owner did have a child from a casual affair in his earlier years and never kept in contact with the mother or her child, he assumed Ted was his biological son.

Since Marsha and Ted filed joint tax returns, and he could not be located, she was liable for all the monies owed to the city, state and Uncle Sam.

She consulted with a tax attorney, and after months of pleading the case, an agreement with all parties concerned was reached. She would only have to pay half of what was owed in property and back taxes.

The original owner of the apartment building got his property back. It took over a year to get all of this turmoil straightened out.

In the meantime, Ted and his sisters were nowhere to be found. It was as though they had evaporated into thin air.

If Marsha thought the worst was over, a shock more painful than an unexpected blow to the head was about to occur.

Once Marsha settled into her new place, it was time for her to take a break from all the madness that had consumed her during the last year. She decided to go to Nassau, made reservations to leave on a Wednesday morning and planned to stay for about two months.

After arriving on the island, Marsha inhaled a mouthful of fresh air, and it felt good. All of her trials and tribulations were behind her. In her exuberant state, she could not wait to get to her oasis. She grabbed a cab and was home in ten minutes. When she got to the door, her key would not fit into the lock.

That is strange, she thought.

There were voices coming from the pool area, and as she got closer, she did not recognize the couple there. A tall woman approached her and asked if she could be of assistance.

"This is my house, and who are you?" Marsha asked.

The woman, with a bewildered look on her face, replied, "My husband and I are the owners of this house."

Marsha stood there as though she misunderstood what the woman said and responded, "I beg your pardon. This house belongs to me; my parents gave me this home as a wedding gift. They were the original owners."

"I beg to differ," the woman said. "My husband and I purchased this house about a year ago from the previous owners; perhaps your parents neglected to tell you this. We have the deed to the house, which I'd be happy to show you." The woman then went into the house, came back and showed Marsha the legal document, establishing the couple as the rightful owners.

"But that's impossible," Marsha said. "I was the previous owner and never sold this house to anyone. Moreover, from whom did you purchase this house?"

"From Ted and Associates."

When Marsha opened her eyes, she was stretched out on the couple's lounge chair. She had fainted and was unconscious for about two minutes.

The woman asked if she should call a doctor, but Marsha declined.

The woman then said, "If you need a place to stay while the ownership confusion is being straightened out, you are welcome to stay in our guesthouse."

After composing herself, Marsha thanked the woman but turned down the gesture and left. Regrettably, she did not have a copy of the deed with her and could not remember where she had placed the document, which named her as the rightful owner, but as she was about to discover, it would not have mattered.

Marsha got a room at a bed and breakfast inn. After settling in, she started to map out her course of battle.

She first went to the realty company that sold the property to Ted and Associates. They showed her documents, which designated Ted as the owner of the house.

However, she never remembered adding his name to the deed. To say she was confused was like saying she was from another planet and could not recall how she landed on earth.

With a copy of that document, Marsha went to the hall of records to file a complaint. If she thought she was going to receive assistance, she was sadly in the wrong.

The clerk could do nothing, because Marsha was married to Ted when she received the house and agreed to give the house to him in the divorce settlement. The clerk showed her the divorce creed, which she had signed, giving ownership of the house to him.

Marsha sat there as though a mallet had knocked her into a trance.

When Ted applied for his quickie divorce in Delaware, he had the lawyer include a clause in the divorce papers that read:

As a final settlement, Ted will receive all real properties obtained before he came into the marriage and all real properties obtained during the years he and Marsha were married.

She signed those papers and remembered reading that paragraph but thought it meant the apartment building Ted had before they met and the parcel of land he was supposedly going to purchase before their divorce. Unfortunately, after receiving those papers, she never consulted with a lawyer, which was an expensive mistake on her part.

Marsha finally woke up. She was the victim of a diabolical scheme, a plot she would have never wished on her worst enemy. Moreover, the deception took place right under her eyes. From the beginning until the end, Ted was setting her up for the big fall.

She tried to figure out how she missed all of the warning signs. She considered herself an intelligent and astute woman. So how could she have missed all of the shenanigans that were going on right under her nose?

But, the biggest bombshell came when Marsha discovered how much money Ted and his perverted sisters got from the sale of her house. It was a windfall of seven million dollars!

It took almost a month for the shock and anger to wear off. There was not much more Marsha could have done. Wallowing or crying was not going to bring her house or the money back. It was now time for her to leave the Bahamas. She got a flight out on a Sunday afternoon and landed in New York late that evening.

Before she stepped off the plane, the talk about her financial mess was traveling around town faster than a speeding bullet.

It was the opinion of many that "Marsha was in a state of unconsciousness while she was married to Ted. What other logical explanation was there that allowed her husband to clean out her trust fund, steal her house and make a seven figure profit from the sale?"

Her parents did not get whiff of the news right away; the couple was on a cruise. They predicted the marriage would fail but never imagined their daughter would end up penniless and homeless.

When Marsha's parents returned from their trip, the scandal hit them like a flash of lightning. Being too humiliated, Marsha would not go into any details with her mom and dad. Since living in her Brooklyn apartment was no longer affordable, she asked if she could move back in with them. Her parents said yes and were as happy as two squirrels eating a ton of peanuts.

Marsha was steadfast; she never wanted to discuss what her ex-husband and sister-in-laws had done to her. Her parents agreed, because everyone in Stuyvesant Heights had already filled them in as to what really took place in the Bahamas.♦

Love, Passion and A Shattered Dream

It was almost nine in the evening when Tawney got home. She was exhausted and landed on the sofa without removing her coat. The long hours at work were starting to take a toll on her wellbeing. She knew it was time to re-examine her situation and add more balance to her life.

For several years, she focused on building a career and was now ready to take that next step, meeting a dynamic man who would sweep her off her feet and take her away from all of the grueling and demanding tasks encountered on the job.

In two years, Tawney wanted to be a wife, have at least two children and be a stay-at-home mom. If her aspirations were going to come true, she would have to start planning her course of action soon.

After receiving her Master's Degree in Computer Science, Tawney immediately got a job at a small tech firm called Tech World, Inc., which was located in Lower Manhattan, New York. She was an educational software developer and worked at the company for over ten years.

There were times when she wanted to pack it all in, because she never felt appreciated by management or her co-workers. Because she was encouraging, hard working and accommodating, the staff would take advantage of her.

When co-workers were on vacation, she would do their work and hers, sometimes putting in twelve hours a day. However, when she went on vacation, her work would pile up, and upon her return, she would end up putting in extra hours and sometimes weekends just to catch up.

Since Tawney was single and had no children, many executives saw this as justification to give her more work. They assumed she had no added responsibilities at home and would welcome the extra overtime. Of course, she never complained about the money.

Her salary was over one hundred and fifty thousand dollars, and with overtime, she was pulling in close to two hundred thousand dollars a year.

In addition, she accumulated a nice nest egg through good investments and savings. Her assets were worth over six hundred and fifty thousand dollars. If warranted, she could have left her job and lived off the interest without touching the principal.

Tawney had always lived in a rent-controlled apartment with her parents, until they retired and moved to Arizona. She remained in the modestly decorated apartment, which was still in her parents' name. Her rent would have been the envy of most of her co-workers; they were paying rents and mortgages in the four figures.

Her sense of style was unfussy. Unlike many of her associates, she had no credit debt, did not own a car and did not live a lavish lifestyle. Living within her means was her strongest suit. She ate out a lot at home and for fun would rent movies or attend off-off-Broadway plays. She enjoyed her successes and was now ready to share those triumphs with someone special.

Tawney was a plus size and sensuous beauty, but her social life would have never made the society pages. She did not date often. Most of the men on her job were married, and the single ones were already in committed relationships.

Although there were a few office romances, she did not believe in mixing business with pleasure and would never date a co-worker. For one thing, people on the job had a tendency to chat about which employee was sleeping with whom. Moreover, some were great at kissing and talking about their colossal lovemaking escapades.

There were even rumors that several male workers were keeping score cards on the number of female employees they were doing. Tawney was a very private person and believed in keeping people speculating about her love life or lack of.

People would always ask, "Are you seeing anyone?"

Her answer would always be, "Not at the moment."

If a male associate asked her out on a date, she would always decline.

Her mother would say, "To be involved with a person you work with is a recipe for disaster, and what goes on in the bedroom should always remain there."

Therefore, Tawney never wanted to come over as being easy or the subject of office gossip or dirty jokes.

However, she was about to ignore her mom's words of wisdom and have an office tryst that would leave her with a crushed heart.

Now that Tawney's career was on track, it was time for her to find a dynamic man. She put in a request for a one-year sabbatical, but the company would only give her six months' leave. She was somewhat thrown, because workers who wanted to take a one-year break could if they were with the company for ten or more years. Nevertheless, she went along with management's decision. If she did not accomplish her goals in six months, there were other options.

Friday was Tawney's last day on the job. Before she left, the staff gave her a going away party and introduced her to the person who would be filling in for her. His name was Jamal. He was a computer software consultant and had his own company called Safety Net Now that designed security software for major corporations and financial institutions.

His company had been around for more than twenty years with annual sales of over five million dollars. He had an assistant and two part-time employees. His business was home-based in Uptown Manhattan.

Jamal was a hottie. Many of the female employees could not keep their eyes or hands off him. To say they were not smitten with his looks would have been incorrect. They flocked around him as if he was the last man on earth.

Tawney appeared to be oblivious to all the excitement.

As the women were talking to him, he was watching Tawney. His alluring smile was beyond description; he was like the worm on the hook, tempting the fish. Without a doubt, he got her attention. His charismatic charm worked, and before anyone realized it, the two were conversing as if they were the only people in the room.

As the party ended, Tawney thanked everyone for the send-off. The staff wished her a great respite and looked forward to her return in six months.

Jamal offered to drive her home, but she declined. She did not want to come over as a fast woman. Even though she was into him, she wanted to play hard to get.

He did ask if he could call her. Of course, she said yes. After all, he was going to be taking over her work and would need to contact her if he had questions or encountered any problems.

After arriving home, Tawney was exhausted and took a warm bath. While relaxing in the tub, she thought about Jamal and romanticized about the two of them being together, getting married, having children and living happily ever after.

The next day, Tawney was up early and started to make plans for the next six months. Suddenly, the phone rang. It was Jamal. He wanted to discuss the work he was going to do while she was on leave and invited her to dinner.

She had no qualms about going out with him and accepted his invitation. He was not an employee of the company. When her sabbatical was over, he would no longer be working there. Furthermore, he did not come over as someone who would discuss his personal business at the workplace.

He made plans to take her out next Friday to a popular restaurant in New Jersey.

She could not wait to see him. Friday could not have come fast enough for her.

In the meantime, Tawney looked through her wardrobe to select an outfit to wear and picked out a nice teal color strapless cocktail dress, a pair of black suede pumps and a hand-made beaded purse to complement her attire.

It was Friday evening. Tawney was getting ready for her date when the doorbell rang. As she opened the door, it was Jamal. When she saw him, a feeling of elation traveled throughout her body. He was drop-dead elegant in his gray pinstriped suit.

She invited him in. When he embraced her, she became aroused but immediately got hold of herself and asked him to have a seat while she finished dressing.

He sat on the sofa, observed her from a distance and had an expression on his face like the cat that just ate the canary.

When she came into the living room, he was speechless. The chandelier could have fallen on him, and he would have never known what hit him.

As Jamal stood up, Tawney got closer. The two cuddled and kissed for almost five minutes and started to make honey like two bees in heat. They ended up in the bedroom and never made it to the restaurant. When he was ready to take a break, she would scream for more. It was almost three in the morning when the lovemaking ended.

When Tawney woke up, Jamal was not in bed; she thought he had left and figured it was a one-night stand on his part. Then she heard a noise coming from the kitchen. As she went to check, he had prepared breakfast. They kissed, and he escorted her to the table. She was thoroughly surprised and impressed.

"Where did you learn how to cook?" she asked.

"While attending college, I worked at a popular Caribbean restaurant in Newark, New Jersey, where I was going to take you for dinner. I worked in the kitchen and learned how to prepare a variety of West Indian dishes from the finest chefs."

If she had any misgivings about him, those uncertainties were eternally gone. She was ready to be his lover and lifetime partner.

After breakfast, the two went back to bed and talked about their years growing up in their respective communities.

Jamal grew up in New Jersey, attended a popular state university and majored in computer science. While in college, he started a business in his parents' basement, designing software for students, local businesses, religious institutions and community organizations.

After graduation, he did freelance work for major tech companies, saved enough money to purchase a brownstone in Harlem and expanded his business to where it was today. Some of his clients were fortune 500 companies, small businesses and not-for-profit agencies. He had just signed on as a consultant with Tech World, Inc.

Tawney talked about her life growing up in Manhattan. She had a sister who lived in Canada. They were not that close because her sister was twenty years older, but Tawney and her parents were extremely close.

Both parents were municipal employees. Her mother was an accountant with the New York City Finance Department, and her father was the head superintendent of several school districts at the Board of Education. After leaving their jobs, they moved to a retirement community to be near family and friends.

Tawney always wanted it all and systematically mapped out her road to success. She graduated from high school at the top of her class and won a full scholarship to a prominent university in Connecticut. She had a steadfast career, accrued lots of money and was now ready to settle down and have children.

Jamal was listening very carefully to what she was saying. Whether he got the message was anyone's guess. As he started to kiss her, his cell phone rang. There was an emergency at his company, which needed his immediate attention. He apologized and said he had to leave.

He got dressed, gave her a loving kiss and said, "I already miss you. Let's get together tomorrow for Sunday brunch at my place, and then we'll go to the restaurant for dinner."

"I wish tomorrow was already here," she replied.

He gave her his e-mail address and cell phone number and said, "I will send a car to pick you up at ten in the morning."

To say Tawney was on top of the world was like saying she was at the peak of Mount Everest and was ready to leap for joy. Sending a car to pick her up was the embodiment of sophistication to say the least. When was the last time someone sent a chauffeur for her? The answer was never! Then again, how often did she date?

Jamal has class. She immediately called her parents and screamed, "I met my future husband."

For a second, her mom who answered the phone did not recognize the voice and thought the person on the other end had the wrong number. As Tawney continued to talk, her mom realized who it was.

Tawney explained in depth how she met the man of her dreams.

Her mother listened and was deeply concerned. Her daughter had only known this man for twenty-four hours. To conclude that he was the one did not make any sense.

Nevertheless, Tawney was madly in love and would marry him in a year.

Her father who was listening in did not voice his opinion. It would not have mattered what he thought. As far as he was concerned, you can never reason with a woman blinded by love. He wished her love and happiness.

Her parents did want to meet this man. Tawney insisted it was not necessary for them to come to New York at this time. It was not as though she was going to marry him next week. There would be plenty of time for her mom and dad to get to know Jamal.

While Tawney was talking to her parents, there was a beeping sound on her end. "There is a call coming in, and I will be talking to you and dad soon."

When she answered the call, the voice on the other end said, "I just called to say I miss you and can't wait to see you tomorrow."

After hearing Jamal's voice, Tawney started to hyperventilate and whispered, "I love you." There was a click at the other end. It was getting late; she was tired, decided to turn in early and had no trouble falling asleep.

It was Sunday, and the church bells were ringing. Tawney knew it was time to get up. She was full of energy and bliss, could not decide what to wear, struggled over several attires and lastly, selected a beige linen pantsuit.

The weather was divine; the temperature was in the mid 70s.

At approximately 9:45 a.m., the doorbell rang. It was the chauffeur, who introduced himself as Rick.

The ride to Jamal's house took about thirty minutes. The driver escorted Tawney to the house and then left. When the door opened, Jamal was in his silk robe and led her into the living room.

The interior of the house was elegant. The four-story residence came with an elevator. The cathedral ceilings stood 16 feet high. There were parquet floors and central air conditioning. The kitchen had all computerized appliances.

Jamal's office, which was on the second floor, had several computers, workstations, printers and scanners. Stored records occupied the third floor, and on the fourth floor were three bedrooms with their own baths.

What Tawney liked most about the house was its beautiful enclosed garden. Believing Jamal had his act together, she was very proud of his accomplishments. He was going places, and she wanted to be by his side.

He took her to his bedroom, which looked more like a love nest. There were several decorative mirrors on the ceiling and imported wall-to-wall black wool carpeting on the floor. Erotic images accentuated the deep red brick walls. On his bed was a zebra skin throw.

Tawney started to get hot. As Jamal got closer to her body, he removed his robe and started to undress her. Before she knew what was coming, they were doing every lovemaking position and technique known to man and woman.

Being in a state of erotic joy, Tawney sensed Jamal was a master of The Kama Sutra or a talisman, who had the power to keep her going and pleading for more. She would have given up all of her worldly possessions and sold her soul to the devil to keep this sensation going.

The aroma from the kitchen was stimulating Tawney's carnal desires. Jamal had prepared hot and spicy cod fish cakes, candied yams, sausages, yellow rice with black beans and coconut bread. She was not hungry and wanted to continue her lovemaking antics with him.

However, he was pooped; they would resume their lovemaking in the evening and instead of going to New

Jersey for dinner, they would eat in. That was acceptable to her. The last thing she wanted to do was go to a restaurant.

That evening, Jamal called and told the driver he was no longer on call. Jamal and Tawney went back to bed and made love until they no longer could.

When Tawney woke up, Jamal was gone. He left a note, reminding her he was going to Tech World. She completely forgot it was Monday, dashed out of bed, dressed and went downstairs.

There was a woman in the living room; she introduced herself as Jamal's assistant.

Tawney greeted the aide and said, "It is nice to meet you."

"Likewise," the woman said.

As Tawney was leaving, the assistant wished her a good day.

"Thank you and you have a great day as well."

When Tawney got home, she made breakfast. While eating, she was thinking about Jamal. Already, she was missing him.

For the next four months, Tawney and Jamal were seeing each other and having wild and romantic trysts.

When she was with him, she was always in a state of sexual glee. To say he had her completely under his control was the truth. He was now ready to proceed with his evil scheme.

The following Saturday, Jamal called Tawney and wanted her input on a business proposal. He was planning to buy a small tech company and asked if she would be interested in becoming his partner; she would only have to invest five hundred thousand dollars. She loved the idea and without even thinking or asking any questions, said yes.

Tawney was excited about the new business venture. While she was going over her portfolio, to decide which stocks to cash in, the phone rang. It was Jamal announcing how the tech company had accepted his bid. All he needed was her share of the money. He instructed her to make the check out to him, personally, and wanted to come by the following Saturday to pick up the money and go over the final plans for procuring the company.

It was now Saturday. Jamal arrived at Tawney's apartment around ten in the morning. She had cashed in three hundred and fifty thousand dollars worth of stocks, borrowed the balance from her 401(k) plan and had a check for five hundred thousand dollars made out to him. It would take about four weeks to finalize the deal.

Tawney started to wonder if it made any sense to go back to work. Now that she was a business owner, management would not take likely to it since there was a clause in her contract that read, *Employees are not allowed to accept any type of employment with any tech company while working for Tech World, Inc.*

While technically, she would not be an employee but a part owner of the new company, it would be a conflict of interest and against policy rules. It was a catch-22, so before making any final decisions, she would consult with Jamal.

In one month, Tawney's sabbatical would end. She still did not know if she was going to return to work.

In the meantime, Jamal finalized the purchase of the new corporation and renamed it Info Limited.

The two celebrated their new acquisition. Jamal asked Tawney to be the C.E.O. of the new company. She was flattered but knew nothing about running a business. She was a software developer and expected to be a silent partner. Jamal told her that he would be her mentor, and she would get assistance from his staff.

When Tawney told him she was planning to leave Tech World, Jamal insisted she remain there for at least several more months or until Info Limited was turning a profit. She thought that made perfect sense; if revenues were slow coming in, she would still have a paycheck to fall back on. Besides, Jamal was planning to leave New York for several weeks to do more acquisitions.

Before Jamal left town, he came to see Tawney and had a big surprise for her. He got down on one knee, took out a four-carat diamond ring and asked for her hand in marriage. She was ecstatic, started to jump up and down like a contestant who just won the grand prize on a game show and accepted his proposal. They got undressed and made intense love into the wee hours of the night. He was leaving the next day, and upon his return, they would plan the most memorable wedding.

For the next couple of weeks, Tawney was craving for Jamal. She had problems sleeping and was tossing and turning every other night. One evening, it was almost one hundred degrees; it was too hot and humid to sleep. She took out her laptop and started to write the following love message:

My Darling Jamal:

As I lie in bed and admire my engagement ring, I am thinking about you more and more each day. Meeting a beautiful, considerate and kind man has always been a vision of mine, and you have fulfilled that dream. You have made me the happiest woman on the planet, and I cannot wait to be your business partner, lover and wife. Hurry home my sweetheart.

Love always,

Tawney

She sent the e-mail to him, closed her laptop and started to make plans for their pending nuptial.

Every other day, Tawney was sending erotic e-mails to Jamal. The fact that he never replied did not faze her at all; she guessed he was too busy to answer. The last thing she wanted to do was throw him off course when it came to making business deals and opted to cool it with the messages. After his return, they would have plenty of time to tease and write notes to each other.

In two weeks, Tawney would return to work and could not wait to tell her colleagues she had met someone and accepted his marriage proposal but would not mention his name or her new business partnership until she was ready to leave.

It was Monday. Tawney was ready to return to work. She woke up feeling excited and arrived on the job earlier than usual. There was a note on her desk, requesting that she come to management's office at once. On her way to the executive suite, there were unfamiliar faces in the conference room.

When she entered the office, her boss, whose name was Thea, greeted her with a vigorous handshake and said, "A company has just bought Tech World, Inc. and renamed it Info Limited, and Mr. Chip Washington is now the new C.E.O."

Before Tawney could declare that she was the C.E.O. and part owner of Info Limited, she received a layoff notice. She sat there in a state of alarm and asked, "Who acquired the company?"

"A multi-national conglomerate located in Seattle, Washington bought-out the firm."

In a confused state, Tawney asked, "Was Jamal part of that conglomerate?"

Thea looked as though she misunderstood the question and asked, "Who is Jamal?"

"He was the consultant who took over my job while I was on leave," Tawney answered.

"Oh yes, now I remember. No, he had nothing to do with the takeover. Besides, he only worked here for four months. There was so much confusion with the buyout and the terminations. I completely forgot about him," Thea replied.

"Didn't he have a tech business of his own?" Tawney asked.

"I am not sure. You would have to ask Human Resources since they hired him," Thea said. She went on to say, how much she enjoyed working with Tawney and how disappointed she was that the new owners did not wish to keep her on. "If it is any comfort, half the staff was fired. When a business goes through an acquisition, there are always cutbacks. You can never take it personally. It is just business," Thea said.

Thea was talking about one thing after another, but Tawney tuned her out. Almost in tears, she thanked Thea, quickly left the building and went straight to Jamal's residence to see what was going on. When she arrived at the house, there was a for sale sign in the front yard. She rang the doorbell but got no answer; she took down the phone number and left for home.

After arriving home, Tawney immediately called the real estate agent. While inquiring about the house, she discovered Jamal never owned the property or the business. He was house-sitting for the owners, who were now living and operating a new business abroad. Jamal and his helper disappeared over a month ago, and no one knew where they were.

The broker did ask if Tawney was interested in buying the property. The asking price was one million dollars in its present condition. It was ironic, because prior to losing her job and handing over her money to Jamal, she might have qualified for a mortgage. Now she barely had enough money to live on.

After Tawney got off the phone, she sat there as though someone had sucked all of the life out of her, that someone being Jamal and surmised his assistant was probably in on the con right from the start.

Jamal used the information regarding the conglomerate's plan to buy Tech Now, Inc. to his advantage and was able to trick her into believing he was purchasing a company. In reality, he was a snake that swindled her out of her money.

How she could have been so dim-witted was devastating. She had very little money and no job and would have to repay the loan, pay taxes and penalties on the money she borrowed from her pension and retirement accounts.

What was Tawney to do next? She was too embarrassed to file a complaint against Jamal. Where would she begin? She knew nothing about this man and reckoned everything he told her was a flat out lie. He used her, pretended to be in love with her and then ripped her off without blinking an eye. Behind that façade was a cruel and immoral person.

Excessively in lust, Tawney never saw the one cautionary sign: Requesting the check for the business be payable to him and not to the company, which was never his from the start.

For the next several months, Tawney was in a state of shock and depression. Every time she went to bed, she would picture being with Jamal forever and seeing the two of them having erotic fun, eventually getting married and having children, but all of her dreams ended up being shattered into miniature pieces. The hurt was just too unbearable. She would cry herself to sleep every night.

After slowly getting over the initial distress, anger and betrayal, she could no longer remain in her apartment or in New York and resolved to move to Arizona to be near her parents. She would have no problems finding work and could probably start her own software designing company. The prospects were endless. She did not intend to tell her parents as to what took place between her and Jamal. That was a tale better left untold.

Before Tawney left New York, she thought about the engagement ring Jamal had given her and decided to go to a high-end jewelry store to have it appraised. The jeweler examined the ring and told her it was a fake.

The appraiser said, "There is a way to tell an authentic diamond. Place the diamond on a business card. If you cannot read the letters, it is real. If you can read the print, you can use the ring as a magnifying glass."

A mortified Tawney ran out of the store and threw the ring into a dumpster.♦

Divine Temptation

By age thirty-two, Shaun was going to be a millionaire and married. He would always hear family members say, "You will never be successful unless you bring others along with you."

He never forgot those words. His objective was to bring prosperity and happiness to others; come hell or high water, his aspirations were going to come true.

Growing up in an urban community and being the youngest of five children, he never saw any signs of hardship. There was always food on the table, and no one ever complained about not having enough money.

Shaun's parents were homeowners and worked in the service industry sector. His father sold life insurance, and his mother was a secretary to the C.E.O. of a major hotel.

The assumption was, if a person owned property and made good money, he or she was doing fine. For all purposes, his family lived a comfortable existence. However, Shaun was never content with just doing fine. He wanted more.

At age eighteen, Shaun graduated from high school and immediately got a job at a high-end women's clothing store in Queens, New York. He started out as a stock clerk, and because of his flair for color and fashion, he would study trends and drop hints on the different designs and accessories that would bring more customers into the store. In three years, he was head salesperson.

When it came to selling, he had the midis touch. With his successful marketing skills, he could have sold feathers to chickens and milk to cows. Whether it was his good looks, the layout of the store or the price tags, women from all over were coming to the shop, so much so, sales literally quadrupled in two years. A year later, he was store manager.

Despite his excellent take-home pay, Shaun was not reaching his goal of becoming rich. He bought lottery tickets and spent over one thousand dollars a year, chasing after an unattainable dream of hitting it big. He had a much better chance at finding UFOs and selling them on eBay; he might have become a millionaire overnight. The way his life was going, he would never become prosperous. He started to re-examine his way of thinking by searching for realistic means of creating wealth.

After twelve years on the job, Shaun came to the realization that becoming wealthy would only come about by being an entrepreneur.

While surfing the Internet for start-up business opportunities, Shaun came across an Internet ministry that offered a home study program; the organization would ordain and authorize people to perform legal weddings and marriage ceremonies in all fifty states.

He had always been impressed with the ministers in his community, and while many of them operated from storefronts, he always wondered how they were able to ride around in expensive cars and wear top name designer threads, while many of their faithful followers were struggling to make ends meet. He speculated the preachers made a great deal of their income performing marriages and figured this would be an ideal business to start. He registered for the course, ordered the ministry's marriage packet and studied the manuals thoroughly. After completing the lessons, he was ordained a legal marriage and wedding officiant.

While doing more research, Shaun decided to launch an on-line matchmaking and marriage service. He would find prospective marriage-minded partners, do pre-marriage counseling, organize and preside over weddings. Couples would have the option to select from three kinds of services.

A simple ceremony would be for couples who just wanted to be pronounced husband and wife.

An informal service would be for couples who preferred to have their wedding in their home or courtyard.

For couples who longed to have their event in a house of worship, banquet hall or on a yacht, they could select a formal procedure.

He would conduct some of the business from his studio apartment and use the shop to attract potential members. When the money started to roll in, he would quit his job and look for larger space.

Shaun's intent was to create a simulated wedding chapel and provide all of the amenities for the bride and groom, such as photography, videography, catering, music and floral arrangements. He even considered starting a travel agency to arrange in person meetings for couples who met through his site. It would be a one size fits all marriage and wedding enterprise.

Since Shaun had the weekends off, he first worked on getting his on-line matchmaking and marriage service into cyberspace. He searched the Internet and found dating software that provided web-hosting, registration of a domain name, e-mail addresses, chat rooms, instant messaging and 24-hour technical support for $99.99 per month. There were no set up or commission fees, and any money he made would be all his.

He named the site Global Matchmaking and Marriage Service or GMMS and asked one of his sales clerks to help set up and design the site.

Her name was Lisa. She had been with the shop for six years and was an expert in computer and Internet technology. She customized the site with an eye-catching logo, added graphics, text, profile questions, terms of service agreement, privacy rules, membership fees and payment methods. To collect membership fees, she advised Shaun to go with a third party e-commerce service. In the near future, he could establish his own merchant account. In lieu of pay, she got the weekends off.

Since the new site had no profiles, Shaun would first have to interview prospective clients and have them complete a questionnaire; he would then upload their profiles and photos to the site. To get women interested in his service, he would offer them a free membership.

Men would have to pay an annual membership fee of thirty-five hundred dollars, which would include a background check, private e-mail address, access to all female members' profiles, chatting, instant messaging and if needed, on and off-line counseling.

Women, who did not have Internet access, would have a code number instead of their home address on their profiles. When a man was ready to contact a female member, his letter with the code number and his contact information would be forwarded to the address on file. The high fee was set to eliminate unscrupulous individuals and attract only serious marriage-minded men.

But little did he know, the deceitful person would not be a man but a mysterious woman who would use her erotic domination and leave Shaun in a state of pandemonium, and if he thought this woman was a she-devil, he was about to discover who the real fiend was.

Since many of the female shoppers were single, divorced or widowed, they would be Shaun's likely candidates to test his service. He had business cards, elegant brochures and colorful flyers printed and instructed Lisa, who worked at the checkout counter, to include the promotional materials discreetly into the customer's shopping bag.

In no time, shoppers were showing an intense interest in joining his service, and the fact that it was free was a blessing. Over two hundred women became members, and more were sure to follow. Word of mouth about his matchmaking and marriage service was spreading faster than a gathering of turkey buzzards searching for their next snack.

In the meantime, Lisa had submitted the site to several popular search engines; soon, GMMS was getting over two thousands hits a week. In its first year of operation, over five hundred men became paying members. The site was now working at full speed.

In its second year, GMMS was getting close to ten thousands visits a week. Men from around the world were joining and connecting with women. More women were signing up faster than Shaun could handle. Before long, he would have to hire someone to keep up with the demand.

He could not believe there were so many lonely people out there, seeking love and companionship and went back to those words his family had told him. He was helping others obtain their dreams of finding a lifetime partner and making good money at the same time.

For Shaun, life could not have gotten any better. He was so busy helping others to fulfill their wishes that he was overlooking his own personal desires: Having a lover and eventually, a wife by his side. He was now thirty-two, unattached and lonely.

To help recruit more female members and manage the busy on-line site, Shaun asked Lisa to be his part-time assistant because she had a great rapport with people. She would work every weekend and receive two hundred dollars. As more money came in, her salary would increase. This gave him more time to pursue other interests. His main goal now was to find a good woman to share in his triumphs.

Many of the shop's employees were starting to become resentful of Shaun's business success. After all, they were not getting a piece of that pie. Word was getting back to the owner, who lived in Hawaii that the shop was a meeting place for lonely men and women. There were also rumors that funds were misappropriated to finance GMMS. These innuendos were of course false, but the talks continued and got uglier. Shaun decided it was time to leave and asked Lisa to come with him.

Since his business was doing so well, Shaun could now afford to move from his small apartment into larger space. He found a nice 1600 square feet split-level loft in Long Island City. It was in a residential and commercial neighborhood; the area was ideal for operating his business, performing marriages and organizing wedding receptions. The rent was reasonable, and he signed a three-year lease.

It took about three months to get the place ready for walk-in business. The loft, which was located on the ground floor, had several work areas.

Lisa had her space, which included a desk, computer, printer, scanner, fax and telephone, and Shaun had a private area for interviewing new members and counseling couples.

In the back were an open kitchen and a spacious dining room that could change into a reception area. The floors were parquet. The ceiling stood twenty-three feet high, and beautiful paintings and wall hangings added a romantic ambiance to the environment. Behind a dividing wall was a replicated chapel.

On the upper level were three bedrooms and three baths. Two bedrooms were honeymoon suites, and the third bedroom belonged to Shaun.

Now that Lisa was a full-time employee, she had more responsibilities, including running the web site and was earning one thousand dollars per week.

Shaun and Lisa had a lot in common. Both were single, motivated and looking for love. She was originally from Atlanta, came from a well-to-do family and was the youngest of three children. She never attended college but was communicative and perceptive when it came to business.

When it came to her sense of style, Lisa had impeccable taste and dressed the part of an executive. If one did not know any better, one would have thought she was the C.E.O. of GMMS.

Besides loving her work, Lisa had eyes for Shaun. Her feelings for him grew stronger each day. He was immensely handsome and a successful businessperson and the fact that he never attended college either was a great achievement. Each day, she was falling in love with him. She was his right-hand person, made the business a winner and dreamed one day of becoming his partner in business and love.

Going into its third year, GMMS was exploding in sales. Shaun was performing marriages every other week. Wedding receptions were being booked a year in advance.

The web site was getting close to five hundred thousand page views a month, and more men and women were becoming members. So far, the business had grossed over eight hundred and fifty thousand dollars. Sales were expected to triple in two years.

The idea of starting or investing in a travel agency was not feasible now. Instead, Lisa arranged for GMMS to be a partner with a popular on-line travel agency whose link she placed on GMMS's site. When a visitor clicked on the link and booked his or her trip and hotel reservations through the travel agency, GMMS would receive a hefty commission and not have to worry about booking trips or reserving hotel rooms for their members.

Lisa's initiative was brilliant, Shaun thought.

Lisa was planning to attend a family reunion and take a well-deserved vacation. Since she would be gone for four weeks, and it was quiet with no immediate planned events, Shaun was able to manage the office and site on his own. If it got too busy, he would hire a temporary worker.

While on the Internet, Shaun received the following e-mail from a singles' bureau in the United Kingdom:

Dear Shaun:

I am the publisher of a monthly matchmaking magazine. My clients do not have Internet access and place their personal ads in this publication. All of their contacts are through snail mail.

The reason why I am contacting you is that I am looking to sell the publication to a company that can distribute it worldwide.

You are a likely candidate because you run a respectable business, and this would be an added feature to your already popular site.

I have read many of the testimonials on your page, and your reputation precedes you. I will be in New York next Friday and plan to stay for one month. Perhaps we could meet and discuss this venture in further details.

Could you recommend a nice place to stay? I look forward to hearing from you. I remain,
Divine Ono, Publisher

When Shaun read that e-mail, he was intrigued, but when he saw her photo, a rattlesnake could have bitten him, and he would have died a happy man. The woman was the epitome of loveliness. For almost an hour, he sat at his desk affixed to her picture. It was as though she had placed a hex on him.

The phones in the office were ringing off the hook, but he was too engrossed with her beauty to hear the sounds. Finally, he came out of his trance and forwarded all calls to his voice mail. The last thing he wanted to do was talk.

He immediately got back to her and wrote:

Dear Ms. Ono:

It was a pleasure hearing from you. I would be delighted to meet with you and discuss the possibility of buying your publication.

If you give me your arrival time, I will send a car to pick you up from the airport.

I have lodging at my loft, and you may stay here as my guest.

Looking forward to hearing from you shortly.
Shaun

Divine got back to him. She would arrive at LaGuardia Airport at two in the afternoon and graciously accepted his invitation to stay at the loft. Lisa was not due back on the job for another two weeks.

On Friday morning, Shaun called in a housekeeping service to get Divine's room ready. Lisa usually took care of those details when out-of-town couples reserved one of the suites for their honeymoon; she would make the room personal and alluring. He gave the team instructions to make the suite hospitable and romantic.

Chocolate covered cherries decorated the pillows; red, pink, and yellow rose pedals accentuated the bed, and scented lit candles filled the bathroom. One would have thought he was planning a night of hot and sultry lovemaking with this woman.

Divine's flight arrived on time. The limousine driver met her at the airport and drove her to the loft. When she entered Shaun's office, the two embraced and exchanged salutations.

"It is a joy to meet you, Miss Ono. Please, make yourself at home. I took the liberty of making dinner reservations for six o'clock this evening at a popular restaurant in Manhattan, unless you prefer to eat in."

"That sounds nice. I am looking forward to having dinner with you in the city. If you could show me to my room, I would like to freshen up, and please, call me Divine."

He agreed and took her to her room. When she entered, a sense of desire overtook her. She quickly unpacked and took a cold shower. After getting out of the tub and drying off, she primped her hair, touched-up her makeup and slipped into a red tight-fitting short dress. She was now ready to play the most diabolical role of her life.

Shaun and Divine arrived at the restaurant, which had an intimate and a quaint charm. As they sat down and ordered drinks, she immediately started to talk about herself.

Born in Cameroon, Divine and her family moved to the UK when she was sixteen years old. She attended college, had planned to major in writing and journalism but dropped out in her sophomore year.

Her first job was as an advertising sales rep at a local weekly singles' newspaper. Several years later, the paper collapsed.

She had received a large inheritance from her father, who died in an unsolved plane crash and started her own dating newsletter. What started out as a plain quarterly twelve-page bulletin grew into a popular and colorful high-glossy magazine.

If Shaun was paying attention to what she was saying, it was not evident. As she continued to discuss the selling points of the publication, he was gazing at her like a vampire ready to take his first bite. Her exquisiteness and exotic features had him salivating as a dog would at the site of food. She enchanted, teased and turned him on, until he could no longer concentrate. Just by observing his body language and facial expressions, she knew he was now under her control.

After dinner, they promptly left the restaurant and hailed a cab. It took about thirty minutes to get back to the loft. Like two horny ticks, they started to undress each other and dashed up the stairs. He picked her up and carried her into the bedroom. They made love for over four hours. She was a sexual force, which he could not resist, or as some folks would say, "She was a feline in heat."

Divine definitely lived up to her name and gave him an awesome and a memorable spiritual awakening. He never experienced these kinds of erotic feelings in his thirty-three years. This woman had more moves than a worm slithering in and out of wet terrain. For hours, he begged her not to stop, and she rewarded him with her carnal maneuvers. Eventually, they fell asleep.

When Shaun woke up the next morning, he knew Divine was going to be his lover and partner for life. He fell for her, as a meteorite would fall to earth, fast and hard.

The two had breakfast and talked more about the magazine. Her asking price was two hundred and fifty thousand dollars. She did not have to twist his arm. He agreed to her offer, asked her to stay on as managing editor and to set up residence in the United States. She had a better idea: "Why don't you move the business to the UK? We could work together as a team."

"What a superb idea," he responded.

She explained how wonderful it would be for him to live and work in the UK. They could expand the magazine along with GMMS throughout the UK market. Office space was inexpensive, and he would not have any problems officiating marriages or getting members to join his service.

She highlighted that over half of the British population had registered on at least two on-line dating sites, while many of them have been on a dating site at some point. A third of those who registered found long-term relationships; a quarter of them were still going strong, and six percent had gotten married. Wow! He was impressed with those statistics and concluded relocating to the UK was the prudent thing to do. The two made tantalizing love until late afternoon.

For the next several days, Shaun and Divine did some sightseeing, took in a play on Broadway, attended a couple of street festivals and shopped along Fifth Avenue. They were having the time of their lives. Two weeks later, he asked her to marry him. She accepted his proposal.

It was now Monday, and Lisa was on her way to work. She could not wait to see Shaun and wondered how he managed without her. After all, she was the glue that held that company together. Her creativity and advertising capabilities were responsible for the company's continuous growth in sales and profits. All she dreamed about was being his lover and eventually his wife. She would have slept on a bed of nails to be with him.

When she walked into the loft, he was on the phone and waved at her; she waved back. After he got off the phone, she went into his office. He welcomed her back, and she gave him a big hug, but his reaction was more professional than personal. He asked her how her family reunion and vacation went.

"Great! I saw family members and friends whom I had not seen in years, but I missed being here with you."

Before he could respond to her, Divine walked into the office and introduced herself as his business partner and fiancée.

With a look of shock, Lisa stood there as though someone had thrown a bucket of ice-cold water in her face; she felt the blood curdling throughout her body. If her fury had any powers, Divine and Shaun would have been burning in hell.

How could he do this to me? Who is this Divine woman, and where did she come from? Lisa asked herself. With a pretentious smile, she replied, "It is a pleasure to meet you, and congratulations on your partnership and engagement. Best wishes to you both."

Lisa walked out of the office, went to her desk and held back the tears.

In a couple of weeks, Divine was planning to return home. She contacted her lawyer to draw up papers for the sale of her magazine. Once she receives the money, Shaun would have the title and the rights to the publication. It would take about one month to complete the deal.

Shaun explained to Lisa how the two met, the agreement they made, how they fell in love and his plans to move to the UK. Sitting there attentively, she had a sneered expression like the tempest in a teapot.

Divine was getting ready to leave for the UK, but before she left, and to make their engagement official, Shaun called her into his office and gave her a two-carat diamond ring. She came out of the office and with a sly smile on her face, approached Lisa and said, "Look at the ring Shaun gave me. Isn't it stunning?"

When Lisa saw that ring, she became more infuriated and in a restrained manner said, "Yes, it is beautiful."

Divine then said, "It was a pleasure to meet you. I hope to see you at the wedding next year."

The next day, Divine left for the airport. When she arrived home that evening, she e-mailed Shaun and gave him her bank account number. Two days later, he wired two hundred and fifty thousand dollars into her account.

Shaun was making plans to move. It would take up to a year to get all of the papers needed to leave. He called Lisa into his office and asked if she would stay on until the business relocated to the UK.

With a phony smile on her face, she answered, "Yes. I will take care of the web site and inform all of our members that the company will be going to the UK, sometime in the near future. Just leave everything to me."

Shaun would not leave until the lease on the loft was up or plan any more ceremonies or events. In a couple of weeks, he would go on leave and return in two months.

Before Shaun left, he handed Lisa an envelope, thanked her for her loyalty and continued support. When she got home that evening and opened the envelope, in it was a bonus check for five thousand dollars.

What an insult. He would give a stranger a quarter of a million dollars but thought very little of my contributions to the success of the company, and to add insult to injury, he is going to marry that strumpet.

Lisa immediately went on-line to do a search on this woman and her magazine. She typed in the name of the magazine; its address and e-mail came up. When she inquired about Divine, no one at the company knew this woman nor was she ever employed by or associated with the publication. *What a pathetic fool Shaun was; how this woman could have so easily taken him in was beyond comprehension,* Lisa thought, laughing.

When Lisa got to the office on Monday, she went on Shaun's computer and checked the account number that received the money. It was located in an offshore account. One week after receiving the money, Divine closed the account.

As Lisa promised Shaun, she was going to take care of business. It would take her three weeks to plan her revenge. Her first line of attack was to check the company's bank account. There was a total of nine hundred and fifty thousand dollars in the account.

What Shaun did not know was that she had set up a dummy corporation and a secret bank account in the Cayman Islands and had the money from GMMS's account wired into hers. She then purchased a plane ticket to fly to the islands, but before leaving, she had several more tasks to accomplish.

She bought hard drive eraser software and got on Shaun's computer, went on-line and permanently removed and closed the web site. She then erased all private files, photos, documents, members' contact information and records pertaining to GMMS and the loft from all the hard drives. Paper files, floppy disks, DVDs and CDs, which stored backed-up files, programs and operating systems, were shredded. Then, she went home and erased all data from her computer.

One week later, Lisa arrived in Grand Cayman, went straight to the bank, withdrew all the money, closed the account and left the island. Only her shadow knew where she went.

When Shaun got back from his vacation and walked into the loft, he called out to Lisa, but there was no answer. He figured she was coming in later.

There must have been over five hundred messages on his voice mail. He thought that was strange, because she would have never allowed calls to gather like that. He decided to call her at home, but the phone was not in service. He started to wonder if something had happened and immediately went to her place in Brooklyn. When he got to the building, he went to her apartment and knocked on the door.

The superintendent approached him and said, "The apartment is empty. Lisa moved out abruptly and left no forwarding address."

Shaun stood there in total disbelief and did not know what to think. He went back to the office, turned on his computer, but the screen was blank. He went to Lisa's workstation, and her screen was blank too.

At this point, he was confused and thought there was a power failure. He went to the file cabinet to retrieve the backed-up disks, but they were gone. At first, he thought there was a break-in, but there was no sign of a force entry, and nothing else was missing.

Expensive equipment lined the office. If thieves were going to steal anything, they would not have just taken disks and software. If he was at a loss as to what was going on, he was about to get the worst shock of his being.

To see what the problem was Shaun called in a technician to examine all the PCs.

The expert informed him that someone had scrubbed the hard drives cleaned of all files, programs and software, and they were irretrievable. The operating system and programs that were previously on the PCs would have to be re-installed. However, this was impossible because all of the recovery, boot disks and software applications were gone.

When Shaun checked his telephone messages, callers were inquiring about GMMS's web site. Paying members wanted to know what happened to the site and if GMMS was still in business. Complaints were coming in left and right, accusing the company of swindling members out of their money.

The building manager sent a warning that two rent checks had bounced, and Shaun had five days to submit payment, or management would evict him. Next, he got a letter from the bank, informing him that the business account had a zero balance.

In a panic state, Shaun left the loft and went to an Internet café to check his e-mail. The box was flooded with criticisms and protests from irate customers who threatened to report him to law enforcement and the Better Business Bureau for fraud.

He sent an e-mail to Divine to explain what was happening. Within five minutes, the e-mail came back with the following message: *Mail could not be delivered. Box is closed.*

It did not take long for Shaun to realize that Divine had conned him, and Lisa had methodically destroyed his company.

He could almost forgive Divine for her cunning conduct, but he could not understand why Lisa had done such an unspeakable and unforgettable act and started to think back to when the staff at the shop had accused him of embezzling money to finance GMMS. He wondered if she was the one stealing the money. By the end of the year, he was impoverished and had to move back in with his parents.

It did not take long for the scandal to get back to the clothing shop about Shaun's troubles. The customers and employees could not stop talking about Lisa being responsible for bringing down Shaun's empire, and a woman whom he met on-line and fell in love with had duped him out of a quarter of a million dollars.

The employees did not know Divine, but what Lisa did surprised no one. Everyone knew she had the hots for Shaun, but he was too blind to see how deep her love for him went, and to have fallen in love with another woman was downright dumb on his part.

Like an ostrich, his head must have been in the sand, many surmised.

Of course, there were those who felt he got just what he deserved, using the shop and the customers to further his business, only to have it destroyed by a scorned woman. Fate dealt him a deserving payback, they concluded.

It took a long time for Shaun to get over the deception and pain caused by these two women whom he trusted so dearly, but one good thing came out of this horrific situation. The ministry that ordained Shaun offered him a position to oversee weddings and marriages at one of their sites in Arizona.

It took almost two years to get his life back on track.

Still single, Shaun is now more cautious about any woman he meets or falls in love with, lives a humble lifestyle but continues to wonder, *Where is Divine, and why did Lisa betray me in such a vile manner?*♦

Intimate Deception

The rain was coming down hard, and traffic was bumper to bumper. It was close to midnight, and Penny was on the road for almost two hours. She never liked driving in the rain and would have premonitions of skidding off the wet road, ending up in a ditch and being all alone for weeks. When checking the weather earlier, there was no mention or sign of rain. It was as though the sky had just burst into tears without any forewarning.

Penny was on her way home from a dinner date with her now ex-boyfriend, who abruptly ended their two-year relationship. His excuse was that she was moving too fast, and he was not ready to take their relationship to the next level. His rationale for breaking up was a complete surprise to her, because she never placed any demands on him. If he wanted to see other women, it was fine with her.

It was almost two in the morning when she got to her residence. By then, the rain had stopped. She parked her car into the building's underground garage, got on the elevator and went straight to her apartment.

Since she was a little girl, Penny wanted to work in the area of medicine. Just about every family member was on some type of medication for health-related problems. The idea of taking a pill to help alleviate pain, cure or manage a disease fascinated her. She wanted to dispense drugs and offer drug-related information to consumers, so she chose to go into pharmacy.

She attended a well-known college in New York State, received her Bachelor's Degree in Pharmacy and got a job as a pharmacist assistant at a neighborhood drugstore. A year later, she took and passed the state exam to become a licensed pharmacist. Several months later, she was head pharmacist at a major pharmacy chain in New York City.

While reading her mail, Penny fell asleep. Suddenly, there was a knock at the door.

Who could that be at this time of night? Penny thought. When she looked at her watch, it was almost 10:00 a.m. When she looked through the peephole, the person on the other end was unfamiliar to her. "Who is it?" she asked.

"It's Ebo, your new next door neighbor. I just moved in about a week ago," the man answered.

When Penny opened the door, a feeling of delight overtook her body. He was undoubtedly the most handsome man she had ever seen. If she were questioning why her ex had dumped her, it did not matter any more, because Ebo had her full attention, and he was going to be her next main squeeze.

However, it would not be long before her plans to be with him would never come about, and if the neighbors were lacking in friendly gossip, they were about to be hit with the biggest scandal that would rock the city to its core.

Standing at the door, Ebo apologized for disturbing Penny so early in the morning. He wanted to introduce himself and let her know he was living in the apartment next to hers, in case she heard noises, and was a businessperson who traveled frequently.

By now, Penny was extremely impressed and wanted to know more about this good-looking man. Being a gracious neighbor, she invited him to dine with her the following evening. With extreme pleasure, he accepted her invitation.

Penny pondered what she was going to serve for dinner. Her cooking would have never garnered any awards. She ate out most of the time or had meals delivered but wanted to make a first-class impression on Ebo. After all, he was a businessperson and well traveled. Serving him a frozen dinner would be lacking in class and a bad reflection on her, she thought.

She decided to call her best friend Lea, who operated a catering service and asked if she would prepare an elegant dinner for two for tomorrow evening. Even though it was short notice, Lea would come up with a special menu.

Lea and Penny met in college and instantly became best friends. Lea majored in Restaurant and International Hospitality and worked at a well-known catering business for several years. After saving enough money, she decided to start her own catering company, which became an overnight success. Many of her clients included celebrities, politicians, corporate executives and business owners. If one ever wanted to have an elaborate banquet, Lea would be the person to call. She told Penny to leave everything in her hands and not to worry about a thing.

The evening had arrived. There was a knock at the door; it was Ebo. As he walked into the apartment, he had the tone of a king. Penny was definitely going to be his queen.

The aroma from the food had permeated the whole apartment. As the two sat down, he complimented her on the table setting. The menu was simple yet elegant and included: Creamed Crab and Spinach Soup, Yam and Pork Supreme, Glazed Carrots, and Strawberry Sorbet topped with Brandy Sauce.

Lea introduced herself to Ebo as Penny's best friend and the server for the evening.

He extended his hand and said, "It is a pleasure to meet you."

"Likewise," she said.

Penny informed him that Lea owned a flourishing catering service and had planned and prepared the dinner at the last minute.

As the two started to eat, Ebo began to talk about himself. He was born in Montréal, Canada and studied marketing and retailing. Ten years ago, he opened his first high-end shop, selling designer handbags and other fine accessories. He now had shops in Hong Kong, where he lived, Dubai, Ghana, Senegal and France. Last year, his business grossed over fifteen million dollars in sales.

In a couple of weeks, Ebo was going to California to meet with a real estate agent to look for commercial space on Rodeo Drive in Beverly Hills, a famous shopping area that attracts both shoppers and tourists, offering some of the most exclusive shops in the country.

The two women were dumfounded. To be in the company of an attractive man was sexy, but to be in the presence of a millionaire was mouth-watering. The odds of meeting a handsome man who was successful and rich were one in a billion. They would meet dynamic looking men, but they had empty bank accounts. Moreover, the wealthy men they did meet were either married or too hard on the eyes. Yet, here you had a man who possessed good looks, class and money. What more could a woman ask for.

It was getting late, and Ebo decided it was time to turn in. He thanked the women for an exquisite meal and asked Lea for her business card. With a devilish smile on her face, she handed him a card with her name and private phone number.

It took about an hour for Lea to clean up and pack her cooking supplies. Penny thanked her for a job well done and paid her. Lea gave Penny a kiss on the cheek and left.

Penny was thinking about Ebo and falling hard for him. As she was getting ready to go to bed, the doorbell rang. It was Ebo in his robe.

"I am sorry to trouble you, but I could not get over that succulent meal your friend prepared. She is an excellent chef, and dessert was just scrumptious. How did you know strawberries were my favorite fruit?"

Penny just stood there in amazement and jokingly answered, "I am a mind reader."

They laughed.

He then asked, "Can you read my mind now and tell me why I am really here?"

"No," she answered.

"It is because I have strong feelings for you, and I did not want to be alone," he said.

Before she could respond, he got closer, started to kiss her and removed her nightgown. Their bodies interlocked like two horny mosquitoes going down for the thrill. She was in such a state of excitement that if an earthquake had occurred, she would have thought it was the ultimate climax.

Ebo was no doubt the best lover she had ever encountered and wondered how he was able to maintain such staying power when it came to his performance in bed. The lovemaking lasted for almost six hours, a record-breaking task for any individual.

It was near noon when Ebo woke up. He kissed Penny, thanked her for a tremendous night and went back to his place. She immediately called Lea and gave her all the magnificence details about her sexual escapades with Ebo.

Lea listened carefully and asked, "Are you falling in love with this man?"

"You bet," Penny answered.

There was some pseudo unease in Lea's voice when she said, "You know nothing about this man; for all you know, he probably has a wife and child and is just using you. You know men who travel a lot always have a woman in every port."

"If he were married, I would know," snapped Penny, who quickly ended the conversation, thanked Lea again for the lovely dinner and would talk to her soon.

For the next several days, Penny and Ebo were visiting each other and engaging in non-stop heavy lovemaking. She was always in a state of eroticism and heated joy; her moaning permeated throughout the apartment, and he was like a coyote howling over his peak acts.

Soon, neighbors started to complain about the racket that was going on all hours of the night. Eventually, management sent a notice, informing the two that their loud noises were disturbing the tenants and asking them to lower their decibels when they were together.

Embarrassed by their piercing carnal sounds, they decided to cool it. In a couple of weeks, they would both be out of town; Penny was planning to attend a management seminar in Minnesota, and Ebo was going to California to check on a location for his shop.

Meanwhile, Lea was making strategic plans to be with Ebo. She was attracted to him and was determined to be his lover. Moreover, she would stop at nothing to get him. It was warfare, and she was not going to let her friendship with Penny stand in the way.

Lea's desire for him must have been telepathic. As she was getting ready to leave her home, the phone rang. When she answered, the voice on the other end said, "Hello, may I speak to Lea? This is Ebo calling."

While listening to him, she became hot; to cool off, she opened the windows.

"Hi Ebo, it's so nice hearing from you; I was just thinking about you. How are you doing?" she asked.

He told her he was going out of town in two weeks and wanted to see her before he left. He was thinking of having a grand opening party for his new store in California and wanted her to cater the affair.

She said that would be great, and if he could come to her place, they could discuss and plan the event. She gave him her address and said, "I can meet with you this evening."

He agreed and could not wait to see her.

The evening could not have come fast enough for Lea. She prepared a nice feast and remembered Penny saying that Ebo loved strawberries. The old adage, *the way to a man's heart is through his stomach*, was going to play out beautifully and have him eating right out of her hands.

There was a knock at the door; it was Ebo, looking beautiful as ever. He brought along a dozen roses and kissed her on the cheek. She took the flowers and placed them in a vase. Wearing a black see-through lace gown and nothing underneath, she invited him to sit next to her on the sofa.

Ebo smelled the food but was too engrossed with her beauty. He was attracted to her and confessed, "I am not planning to have a catered affair but wanted to see you, because I could not stop thinking about you."

"I have those same feelings about you," she said.

Before saying another word, he removed her nightgown; she undressed him, and they went at it like two gymnastic players in an extreme competition. She was in paradise erotica, and he was in his grandeur. They could scream and moan at the top of their voices, because she lived in a soundproof home. There were no meddlesome neighbors to rain on their parade.

The two took a reprieve and ate dinner. After dessert, they resumed their lovemaking into the wee hours of the night.

It was around eleven in the morning when Lea and Ebo woke up. She was definitely falling in love and wanted to be with him forever. As she was preparing breakfast, he began talking about his planned trip to California.

She interrupted him and said, "Perhaps I could go with you. Many of my clients live there, and I could introduce you to them; they can be potential customers of yours. The rich and famous are forever searching for the next big ticket item."

He sat there in amazement and thought, *What a good business partner she would make. With all of her connections, I could probably open up several shops.*

Ebo took Lea's suggestion. They went back to bed and went at it like two hyenas in lust. He now had her under his control, and in two weeks, he would put his Machiavellian tactics into play.

Lea's catering business was grossing over two million dollars a year. Her home was her headquarters. All business and food preparations took place respectively from her office and spacious kitchen. For large banquets, she would use a commercial kitchen.

When it came to running the business, planning, preparing and cooking elaborate cuisine, Lea was an ace. She had bookings almost two years in advance, but soon her business logic would lapse and cause her downfall.

Lea started to wonder if going into business with Ebo would be the epitome of her accomplishments. She could connect him with the movers and the shakers. It would be a business and love match made in heaven. She concluded that marriage was the next step on her agenda. As husband and wife, they would be a force in the business world.

While these ideas were racing through her head, the phone rang. It was Ebo. He had a brilliant plan and wanted to come over and brainstorm with her this evening. She was eager to see him, again.

In the meantime, Penny was making plans to go to her seminar. She was leaving the next morning on an eight o'clock flight to Minneapolis. Before departing, she wanted to spend the night with Ebo, but he came up with an excuse. "I'll be tied up this evening with a client and won't be home until after midnight."

She had no idea he was going to be with Lea.

He told Penny how much he loved her and had a couple of hours to spare. She went to his place, and the two ended up in bed and went at it like a tiger and tigress participating in wild sensual acts. It would be her last ultimate and physical enjoyment with him. Before she left, he reminded her he would be out of town for the next three weeks on business.

"I will be back before you. Have a safe trip, my darling," she said.

"And you as well, my love," he said in an underhanded pitch.

When Penny left his apartment, Ebo called Lea and said, "I'll be at your place in one hour." He started to pack his bags and would leave New York the following night.

Around six in the evening, Ebo had arrived at Lea's place; she was like a rattlesnake, ready to engulf him and never let him go. She played right into his hands. Being so elated, she had no idea what was coming. He brought along a bottle of wine and poured them both a drink; they stood up and toasted each other. As they sat back down, he started to talk about an investment idea, but she passed out.

When Lea woke up the next day, she was in a daze and heard Ebo saying, "Good morning, my dear. Did you sleep well? After the long talk about our business partnership last night, you fell asleep. We do not have much time to waste. I must get the money before I leave for California. My flight leaves tonight at nine. As we discussed last night, you will wire one million dollars into my account; the transaction will take about four weeks to finalize. My real estate agent assures me that in six months, the new shop will be up and running. You and I will get married, set up residence in California but live in Hong Kong for most of the year."

When Lea heard those words coming from Ebo's mouth, a feeling of exhilaration overtook her. Since she had an on-line bank account, it would be faster and more convenient to do the transaction. He gave her his account number, and she merrily logged on and had one million dollars wired into his account.

The two were so overjoyed and went back to bed. If she thought there was going to be extreme lovemaking, it would never take place. After consuming more wine, she was sleeping like a baby. It would take weeks before Lea would come out of her state of confusion.

Two weeks had gone by, and Penny was due back from her seminar. She missed Ebo so much that concentrating during the workshops became unbearable, but she managed to get through the classes and in-group discussions.

Sharing what she learned from the meetings with management was not going to be easy. When she got back to work, longing for Ebo became her preoccupation, so much so, she made several errors when filling prescriptions. Lucky for her, one of the pharmacists caught the blunders.

Penny decided to take some personal days before she found herself on the unemployment line or worse, a defendant in a negligence suit. She called Lea but kept getting her voice mail. *Lea's a busy bee*, she sensed.

It was near the holidays and the busiest time of the year, so it was understandable why Lea did not return Penny's calls. She decided to turn on the TV. All of a sudden, she heard a noise coming from Ebo's apartment. *He is home early from his trip*, she thought.

She rushed over to his place and knocked on the door. A woman answered. At first, Penny thought the woman was the housekeeper. "Hello, may I help you?"

"I thought Ebo was back from his trip."

"Mr. Ebo left two weeks ago. He signed a one-year rental agreement but ran out on the lease and left the owner hanging," the woman said, looking perplexed.

If Penny was confused, she was about to become more puzzled and asked, "Where did he go?"

The woman could not give her any more information. Her job was to come in and set up the place for the next tenant.

Penny did ask if she could get in touch with the owner of the apartment. The woman gave her a number to call. She thanked the woman, went back to her apartment and made that call.

The owner informed Penny that Mr. Ebo was to live in the apartment for one year but unexpectedly left, provided no reason and no thirty-day notice. When she inquired about his former address, the owner refused to divulge that information. She thanked the man, hung up and started to cry.

By now, Lea was slowly coming out of her mesmerizing state. For a split second, she started to call out to Ebo but remembered he was in California attending to business. Somehow, she was having short-term memory gaps as to what had taken place during the previous two weeks. All she remembered was sipping wine with him.

When Lea went to the phone, there were over one hundred messages. As she listened, several were from Penny, and the remaining calls were from clients and vendors, requesting confirmations and down payments for upcoming events. To say she was in a state of disorder was an understatement. She assured each caller that arrangements and preparations for future events were moving forward and started writing checks to the various vendors.

There was a big ceremonial dinner coming up in one week. Lea had ordered the supplies and food and hired extra staff to help with the catering. Everything was going efficiently. Then, the unthinkable happened.

Merchants were calling and complaining that checks were coming back stamped insufficient funds. She knew that was impossible, because there was over one million dollars in her business account. The bank must have made an error.

She immediately went on-line and discovered there was only one hundred dollars in her business account and nothing in her savings or checking accounts. She ran to the bank, became hysterical and accused the bank of stealing her money; she threatened to call law enforcement. She was so loud, a crowd started to gather.

After calming Lea down, the bank manager pulled up her records, which showed she had wired over one million dollars to an offshore bank account about two weeks ago. She insisted no such transaction took place and wanted to know where this account was located.

The manager checked and said, "As soon as the money was received, the account was closed by a Mr. Ebo."

Lea hollered, "Ebo! How could you do this to me? Why did you deceive me in such a despicable manner? I trusted and loved you with all my heart."

The manager then said, "It sounds like you were swindled by this man. My advice to you would be to file charges against this person, but it will be difficult to track this individual. These crooks disappear once they get the money. Most often, they are using fake identities, and if they are operating in a foreign country, you may not have any recourse for getting your money back. The law has no jurisdiction in another country. I am truly sorry for your loss."

Lea left the bank in a distraught state. After arriving home, she sat on the couch in a fetal position and wailed uncontrollably.

Most of the neighbors in Penny's apartment building knew Lea, whose reputation as a top-notch caterer preceded her. They were also aware that she and Penny were best friends. Thus, it did not take long for the news to get back to Penny about Lea's misfortunes.

A group of neighbors stopped Penny as she was coming into the building and told her about Lea going berserk in the bank. Their take on the situation was that she was fooling around with a man name Ebo, and he conned her out of one million dollars. When Penny heard this, she could not believe her best friend would betray her in such a manner.

Many of the neighbors had no idea the man in the apartment next to Penny's was Ebo. They knew she and the tenant were doing each other. After all, they were the ones complaining about the ruckus that was coming out of their apartments.

Some neighbors never really knew who was living in that apartment and rarely saw anyone going in or out of the place, until he arrived. When they saw Ebo, people assumed he was the new occupant.

Neighbors had a tendency to keep to themselves and tend to their own business, but that all changed when the scandal erupted; all of a sudden, residents were chitchatting like old bosom friends.

Rumors started to surface that Lea was doing her best friend's boyfriend and bad karma descended on her. The talks became more vicious and vile. Many of her clients accused her of thievery. Her competitors rushed in to take her customers away and started to distribute flyers, offering discounted banquets to those left without a caterer for their upcoming affairs. Cancellations were coming in fast and furious.

There was even an article in a community newspaper accusing Lea of putting out false statements about how Ebo took her money. Instead, the writer suggested, *She hid that money to dodge Uncle Sam*. The finger pointing just added more fuel to the fire.

By now, Lea had fallen on hard times. Her bills were escalating, and she was falling behind in her mortgage payments. She was too embarrassed to face Penny who was avoiding her like the plague.

Civil suits were popping up faster than locusts swarming over crops. The problems were so overwhelming that Lea had disappeared. Many wondered where she went; for all purposes, she was broke and on the streets.

After months of anguish, Penny got over Ebo's dishonesty and Lea's deceitfulness, but she could have been the one financially ruined. Fate was on her side.

Because Lea had more money, Ebo went for the one who had the most. In the end, neither woman won. Penny ended up with a short-lived broken-heart, and Lea was gone.♦

Web of Pretense

Mark was planning to retire from his twenty-five year stint as a high school teacher in upstate New York. In two weeks, it would be his last day on the job. He always knew his calling was to teach.

He received his BS Degree in Math and a MS in Education. Following graduation, he immediately got a job teaching algebra, calculus and geometry at a public high school and spent the best years of his life shaping the minds of young people.

Many of Mark's students went on to attend prominent colleges and universities and became power brokers in business, law, politics, medicine, construction, science, arts, sports and entertainment.

Because of his teaching style and commitment to education, he garnered much respect and admiration from his students and peers. Voted teacher of the year for three consecutive years, he now sensed it was time to leave and pursue other interests.

After consulting with his financial advisor, Mark knew he would be able to live comfortably on his pension and investments. His portfolio, which included stocks, bonds and mutual funds, was worth about three hundred and fifty thousand dollars.

His house, which he was planning to sell, had an assessment value of four hundred and twenty-five thousand dollars, but despite all of his accomplishments, he felt isolated and unfulfilled in his love life.

Mark got married at a young age, but the union ended before it got started, and even though he dated often, there was never a deep love or emotional connection with any of his dates. A few of his friends and co-workers would arrange blind dates for him, but the sparks were never there.

Most of the women he dated were middle-aged divorcees or widows who were unadventurous or set in their ways. Gathering around the table, snacking on munchies and gossiping about who knows what were the ultimate high for most of these women.

Mark enjoyed going to the nightspots and being around energetic people. It was definitely time for him to meet someone who was active and enjoyed doing the things he cherished. If he did nothing else, he was going to find the love of his life and live blissfully ever after.

It has been one year since Mark left his job. He was busy getting his house in order and putting it up for sale. He had lived in his home for over twenty years. He thought about leasing the house and giving the renter the option to buy, but after careful consideration, he decided to sell the property.

He did not want to hold a mortgage or put any more money into upgrading the place as was suggested by the real estate agent. Since the house was already in superb condition, Mark felt selling the house as is would be a better choice.

Mark was very meticulous in maintaining his property, which was a two-story townhouse with three bedrooms; each room came with its own bathroom; there was a spacious kitchen with all modern appliances, a finished basement apartment with its own bathroom and a two car garage, just to name a few of the house's selling points.

The eclectic community included professionals, entrepreneurs, artists, working class people, retirees, young couples and single parents. Then, you had those few individuals who stood around all day doing nothing. It was never quite clear how they made their living, but they were unquestionably the town criers of the neighborhood; if you ever wanted to know what the latest hearsay was, you would go to them.

When Mark bought the house, he was contemplating on being married with children. However, as fate would have it, getting married again was yet to happen. For one person, the house was just too much. In earlier years, some of his relatives were living with him. Ultimately, they purchased their own homes or relocated to various parts of the world.

The homes in his community were appraised from four hundred thousand dollars to six hundred thousand dollars. He was asking for four hundred and fifty thousand dollars. He bought the house for ninety thousand dollars in the mid 1980s and stood to make a nice return on his investment.

Living abroad has always been Mark's dream. He was thinking about relocating to Bermuda, because he had traveled there on many occasions and loved the friendliness of the people, the warm climate and the tranquility, but before making any decisions about moving overseas, he would first have to do more research and find a buyer for his house. This was going to take time, because the housing market was in a deep slump.

Now that Mark had more leisure time, he went on the Internet to check out the latest trends. While he was teaching, going on-line for fun was of no interest to him. He would use the Internet to do research on teaching concepts and new theories in mathematical calculations.

He always encouraged his students to use the Internet as an educational tool but pointed out that they should never rely on the World Wide Web as their only source for acquiring knowledge.

As Mark was browsing through cyberspace, he came across a social networking site for professionals who were looking for dates, romance and fun. He would always overhear some of his associates talk about meeting people for love and other activities in these communities but never gave it much thought.

He never had problems meeting women; he just could not find one with passion and sensuality. He decided to check out the site, started to read some of the women's profiles and became amazed by the number of females who were searching for men.

The majority of the posters were in their early to mid-twenties; Mark was in his early fifties and thought most of the women would have no interest in him. Yet, he did have a youthful-looking face; while teaching, he was often mistaken for a student. All the same, he uploaded his photo along with the following information:

My name is Mark. I am a recently retired math teacher, who has been searching for Miss Right all my life and believe that extraordinary woman is somewhere out there. I am 5'11" tall, and even though I am in my early 50s, I am in excellent physical form and have the stamina of a 20 year old. My goal is to meet a down-to-earth, loving and caring single female for a relationship, leading to marriage. I am compassionate, romantic, kind, financially secured and enjoy traveling, dinning out and going to nightclubs. Your looks, social or economic status is unimportant. If you are interested, please drop me an e-mail.

While Mark was at his computer, he started to reminisce about his coming of age in New York State. He and his younger sister were born in the 1950s, in a close-knit community. His parents were physicians and instilled in their children the importance of education. He always loved and excelled in numbers, so he became a math teacher. His sister was a surgeon who lived in Ghana with her husband and three children.

He met his first love during his sophomore year in high school. Her name was Keisha. She was a beautiful and popular girl. From the day they met, everyone dubbed them the perfectly matched couple.

After graduating from high school, Mark attended an out of state university, while Keisha went to a college in New York City. They made a promise to remain faithful to each other, because they were planning to get married after completing their studies.

The two would see each other during spring and summer breaks, but when she got pregnant, he thought she was carrying his child. He dropped out of college and married her. Then rumors started to surface that while he was away at college, she was seeing and sleeping with his best friend, Hank, and the child she was carrying was not Mark's baby.

People in the neighborhood figured it out but started to question how Mark, the math whiz, had miscalculated the month of conception as to when the baby was born. It was numerically and humanly impossible for Mark to have been the father, because Keisha got pregnant while he was away at school.

After the baby was born, a blood test proved that Hank was the biological father. The fact that Keisha had betrayed Mark was bad enough, but to have slept with his best friend was the ultimate disloyalty. Mark filed for an annulment and went back to school to finish his studies.

A month later, Keisha and Hank got married, and the couple along with their infant daughter left New York for parts unknown. Mark never saw or heard from them again.

Mark often thought about the couple and wondered if they were still together but concluded, if Keisha cheated on him, she was probably unfaithful to Hank. It was now getting late. He logged off his computer and turned in for the night.

It has been a week since Mark posted his profile on the social network. It was Saturday morning and snow had started to fall. He decided to stay in for the day and went on his computer to see if there were any responses to his posting. He received an e-mail with an attached photo. The message read as follows:

My name is Misty, and your personal ad really touched me. I am 25 years old and very outgoing with a dynamic personality. I enjoy having fun, traveling, cooking and reading. Age is nothing but numbers, so the fact that you are in your 50s is a complete turn-on to me, because I love being spoiled and pampered by an older man. I am a licensed cosmetologist and plan to open my own spa shortly. After looking at your photo, it is hard to believe that you are over 50. You do not look a day over 30. Meeting and getting to know you would be my pleasure. I am temporarily residing in Arizona and planning to move soon. Looking forward to hearing from you. Bye and be well.

After reading that e-mail and looking at her photo, someone could have hit Mark over the head with a cast iron pan, and he would have never felt the pain. He started to feel like a teenager, having his first crush. To say he was not smitten with Misty's beauty would have been a false proclamation.

She had the face of an angel and a body that could make a man's head twirl, even if his cranium was stuck in cement. Just from that snapshot alone, he knew she was the woman for him. There was no doubt about it. She was going to be his partner for life. He quickly got back to her, and for the next couple of months, the two were e-mailing and chatting like star struck lovers.

What Mark did not see coming was that his obsession with finding love and joy would bring about a devious plan, which would wipe him out financially and leave him emotionally destroyed. Moreover, if the community was lacking in gossip, it was about to be hit with the biggest scandal that would leave folks buzzing like bees making honey.

Just about every other day, Mark and Misty were talking on the telephone. She was planning to purchase a spa in Albuquerque, New Mexico and needed help in deciding if investing in such an endeavor would be a wise move.

The asking price for the health spa was eight hundred thousand dollars and came with all the equipment and supplies to get started. The location was ideal because it was a great tourist attraction.

Misty wanted to purchase the business right out rather than take on a mortgage. Having most of the money, she would borrow the rest.

Mark had no experience with this type of enterprise but thought the idea was brilliant. Wondering if relocating to New Mexico was the answer, he invited her to come to New York. They would discuss the undertaking and come up with a plan. She promptly accepted his invitation. He purchased an open-ended plane ticket for her, and in two weeks, she would be in New York.

Mark was getting the house ready for Misty's arrival. He went to the store to stock up on food and other items. For the very first time, he did not feel unfilled or alone. When he got back home, there was a flyer in his door, which read:

Astrology Reading by Grace - Consults and advises on all matters, such as love, marriage and business. All readings are private and confidential.

What a coincidence, he thought. After all, he was about to take on a new love interest, a major business undertaking and a possible marriage. *Is this a sign that my life is finally going in the right direction?* Suddenly, he became excited, and the next day he paid the woman a visit.

When Mark entered Grace's establishment, an elderly and cordial woman greeted and escorted him into a tiny room in the back of the storefront. Her specialty was palm, tarot and psychic readings and examining numerology, crystal and astrology charts. Since this was his first time visiting this type of venue, he was baffled as to which reading to have.

"What matters are of interest to you?" Grace asked.

He told her he had just met the woman of his dreams; she was interested in buying a business, and he wanted to know what the future had in store for the two of them.

Grace recommended the special reading, which cost thirty-five dollars. Mark agreed and handed her the money.

The psychic foresaw his fate and predicted, "You are making the right decision when it comes to your love life; you will provide financial assistance to your mate whose first name begins with the letter M; the salon, which she plans to buy, will be successful beyond your wildest dreams. After you sell your house, you will move somewhere in the southwest, tie the knot and have beautiful children."

Mark was completely stunned. *How could this woman have known all of this? She was right on the mark about the spa, the possible move to New Mexico and an imminent marriage.* He thanked Grace and left feeling more electrified and knew what he had to do next.

In a few days, Mark was expecting Misty to arrive in New York and was planning to meet her at the airport. He was upstairs, tidying up and putting the final touches in the guest room; unexpectedly, the doorbell rang.

When he went downstairs to open the door, it was Misty. To say he was in a state of shock was no lie. They hugged and kissed each other as though they were lovers who had not seen each other for years.

"Why didn't you call me from the airport?" he asked.

"I wanted to surprise you," she said, and a bolt out of the blue it was.

Nevertheless, both were thrilled to meet.

He asked her how her flight went.

"It was a smooth and pleasant ride."

They talked a little bit. He then showed Misty to her room; she would unpack and freshen up before joining him downstairs.

Misty loved her room; it had its own bathroom, which was an additional benefit. The house was elaborate; she figured it could sell for at least four hundred thousand dollars.

Mark is as handsome in person as he is in his photo, she reflected. From all of his e-mails, on-line chats and phone conversations, she read him like a paperback and recognized that he would swim through shark-infested waters to have her in his life. She observed the desperation in his face, studied his body language and knew he would be an easy mark. *No pun intended*, she thought, giggling and was now ready to put her malevolent plot into full drive.

While Misty was in her room, Mark was preparing dinner. He could not remember being in such high spirits. When he saw, embraced and kissed Misty, he finally sensed the fire works, a love connection and vibrations that he never experienced with any woman, not even with his first love, Keisha. He thought about what the psychic foresaw and whispered, "Grace definitely got it right. Misty is going to be my wife."

Mark was an excellent cook and could have been a top chef at any restaurant. *Perhaps, when Misty opens her spa, I could prepare nutritious gourmet meals for her clients.* He had so many bright ideas and could not wait to share them with her.

Dinner was almost ready. Misty smelled the aroma coming from the kitchen and came dashing down the stairs. She wore an outfit, which shouted make love to me!

When Mark saw her, he wanted to carry her back up the stairs, into the bedroom and make passionate love to her, but he remembered something from their conversations. She did not believe in pre-marital sex and was saving herself until she got married.

Besides, Mark was old school; unless she made the first move, he would have never made advances towards her. Little did he know that move was never going to come.

The two sat down and started to eat. Misty praised him on his exquisite meal. After dinner, she offered to help with the cleanup, but being the man he was, Mark declined. Before long, he joined her in the living room, and they chatted for hours. At times, they would laugh, kiss and hold hands. As he looked into her eyes, there was a familiarity about her; she reminded him of Keisha.

Just as Mark had talked about his life, Misty conversed about growing up in Arizona with her mother, who was divorced from Misty's father. He was a retired telephone technician living in Alaska with his current wife. She did not have much contact with her dad and was on bad terms with her mother. They had not spoken or seen each other for over five years.

After graduating from high school, Misty attended cosmetology school and went on to acquire her license. For the next several years, she worked as a consultant at high-end department stores, doing makeup applications and teaching skin-care techniques to their up-scale clientele. She always wanted to be her own boss; she was the beneficiary of a five hundred thousand dollar insurance policy and decided to purchase a spa from a business associate in Albuquerque.

The spa would sell a line of cosmetics and skin-care products, do body wraps, hair styling and nail sculpturing and conduct workshops on applying makeup and ways to maintain a healthier and younger looking skin. She showed him her business plan. He read it and quickly signed on to assist her.

When Mark said he would relocate to New Mexico, she quickly said, "The agent managing the acquisition of the spa can find the ideal place for us."

Mark would cash in some of his stocks and bonds to help buy the health resort, put his house on the market, and the proceeds from the sale would go toward buying a new home in Albuquerque.

It was now Monday. Mark called his broker, gave him instructions to cash in most of his stocks and bonds and to wire the money to his bank. A week later, he went to the bank and had a cashier's check made out to Misty.

That evening, Mark asked Misty to marry him. With a fake shock on her face, she accepted his proposal. He then handed her an envelope, and in it was her engagement gift: A check for three hundred thousand dollars.

She kissed him and said, "Thank you, my love. You do not realize how happy you have made me!"

"I do, because you've made me the happiest man on earth."

Misty mailed the check to her real estate agent and told Mark it would take a couple of months before the title to the spa would be in her possession.

Mark contacted his real estate agent and said, "If you can find a buyer now, I will come down on the asking price." The following week, the agent had scheduled an open house for potential buyers.

Meanwhile, Mark and Misty were celebrating their engagement and business venture. The two were eating out just about every other day, checking out some of the local nightclubs and playhouses, shopping at the strip mall, kissing, laughing and holding hands and acting like teenagers going through a puppy love phase. To say they were not having the time of their lives would have been false.

By now, talk was spreading quickly that Mark was seen flaunting around town with a woman who was young enough to be his daughter.

Some went so far to say, "He was her sugar daddy."

Yet, those who knew him well could not believe he would be attracted to someone half his age. A few thought he was going through a mid-life crisis and the fling was just a passing moment. Many of the women he dated, in his earlier years, wanted to know where he met this person, and who was she.

When folks found out the two were getting married and planning to live in New Mexico, everyone was at a loss for words. It was as though the cat had gotten their tongues, but soon, those tongues would be wagging faster than a dog's tail.

The real estate broker found potential buyers for Mark's house. They were a couple with two children. The wife operated a children's daycare center, and the husband was the C.E.O. of an executive recruiting and staffing firm. They walked through the house and fell in love with it. For them, the house and the neighborhood were idyllic for a growing family.

The couple bid four hundred and fifty thousand dollars for the house. The offer was accepted, and the husband and wife were now the proud owners of a beautiful home.

Mark and Misty had thirty days to vacate the property. She decided to return to Albuquerque to check on the spa and scout around for a new house. He felt this was a good idea since it would take time for him to tie-up loose ends.

A week later, Misty e-mailed Mark; she found a beautiful three bedroom, three-bath duplex in a luxury-gated community, not too far from the spa. The asking price was three hundred and ninety-five thousand dollars. It had a private courtyard and a terrace overlooking the city. There was tile throughout the place. The spacious kitchen was equipped with stainless steel appliances, granite countertops with tile backsplash and alder custom cabinets. There were solid stained wood doors, a 23 feet foyer, a roof tile and many more fine add-ons.

He saw a video of the house and was extremely pleased with her selection. She had an eye for beauty and excellent taste. As long as she loved the place and was happy, he was happy. A week later, Mark mailed her a cashier's check for four hundred and ten thousand dollars. The extra money would cover closing costs, purchasing furniture and other accessories for the new home.

The new owners had finally moved into Mark's house. He was staying at the YMCA and preparing to leave for New Mexico.

Four weeks went by, and Mark had not heard from Misty. He figured she was busy getting the spa ready for its grand opening, furnishing and decorating their new home. He decided to call her, but the number was disconnected. Of course, he concluded that she was probably at the new residence, but he neglected to get the name and phone number of the real estate agency that was handling the sale.

Mark went on-line and sent an e-mail, but Misty never replied. He wrote a letter to the address where he had mailed the check, but one month later, the envelope came back stamped *Unclaimed*. He had no idea where the house and spa were. For all he knew, they were in Timbuktu.

Two more months flew by, and Misty never contacted Mark. He decided to call the Albuquerque police department to file a missing persons report. After he explained the circumstances and before he could finish his conversation, the officer on the other end knew instantaneously that Mark was the victim of a hoax.

Finding this con artist would be difficult or virtually impossible. The police could not help him. They did not have much to go on. After all, Mark knew nothing about this woman. He met her in cyberspace, fell for and ended up inviting her to his home, only to discover that Misty was not her real name. The police did advise him to file a complaint with the Attorney General's Office and hire a private investigator.

Mark had just enough money to pay his rent and bills and certainly did not have the resources to hire a private eye. Sitting in his room, he started to shake and weep frantically until there were no more tears to shed.

It did not take long for the community to hear about Mark's turmoil, but the biggest shock came when a local newspaper published an article along with a photo resembling Misty. According to the piece:

This individual is wanted, in a couple of states and abroad, for fraud, identity theft and impersonating a female, and up to now, no one has been able to accurately identify this person, because he uses countless disguises; this photo is the last known image of him, and if anyone has any information, contact the local authorities at once.

Well, the gossip was non-stop. People could not comprehend how Mark could not tell the difference between a male and a female. Many wondered if he was questioning his own sexuality and into the experimental stage. Some went so far to say, "He went both ways."

However, what folks did not know was that Mark never slept with Misty or saw her naked. Every time he saw her, she always wore makeup and was completely clothed.

Her hair color and hairdo were somewhat different from the newspaper's depiction, but she had an air of secrecy that left everything to the imagination, and this was one of the attributes that he loved the most about Misty. In his mind, she was a female because there were never any signs that implied she was not.

When Mark read the article and saw that photo, he became emotionally and physically ill.

People would look at him as though he were an extraterrestrial from planet Neptune. A few of his neighbors would avoid or not speak to him, and many started to feel sorry for him.

Some of the women, whom he dated in the past, could not stop talking about or laughing at him. They joked about his intent to marry a younger woman who turned out to be a man as the icing on the cake. It was as though these individuals were getting their revenge, because he did not find them desirable but fell for what he thought was a sweet young thing. Instead, she ended up being an old man's boy toy. It was poetic justice.

As Mark looked back on his life, it was a self-fulfilling prophecy that deception came knocking at his door, again. *What signs did I radiate that allowed people like Keisha and Misty to use me in such a low way? What was it about me that attracted these types of people into my life?* he wondered.

The answers to those questions would probably take years to answer. He was so obsessed with finding love and happiness that all of his common sense and instincts went out the window. Still, he believed misfortunes do occur for a reason, and perhaps he could help others avoid making those same costly mistakes. He was determined to pick up the pieces and go on with his life and considered going back to teaching or starting a math tutoring program. The opportunities were endless. It was not going to be easy, but starting over never is.

One day, while Mark was taking a stroll, he happened on Astrology Reading by Grace. In the window was a sign that read: *Storefront for Rent*. He stood there for a moment, laughed loudly and headed home.♦

Internet Romance

Kamani has not been in a serious relationship with the opposite sex for several years. Burned so many times and almost giving up on finding true love and romance, she questioned if Mr. Right would ever come her way. Most of her female friends were happily married and those who were not were forever complaining how hard it was to find eligible bachelors.

Always feeling out of place at functions where there were mostly couples and never believing she had much in common with her married associates, she often envied them because their lives and conversations perpetually centered on their husbands and children. For her, it was like looking at their existence through a window or having a minor role in a popular soap opera.

At age twenty-two, Kamani obtained a BA Degree in Graphic Arts Design and went on to complete her Master's Degree in Business Administration from a well-known university in New York City. She went back to California and got a job at a firm that designed and printed posters for large media outlets. After working at the company for over fifteen years, she left to start her own business.

Because of her on-the-job experiences and contacts, Kamani decided to start a design and printing service out of her home; she inherited the house from her parents. She would design and print greeting cards, posters, flyers, catalogs and brochures for small cottage industries, churches and non-profit organizations in the Oakland community. Since her major was in business, setting up the company was a breeze.

It took about two years for the business to get off the ground. Many of her clients came through word of mouth and from advertisements placed in community newspapers.

In its third year of operation, the business generated over two hundred thousand dollars in sales. She expected revenues to double in two years. With all of her accomplishments, she was still lonely.

Finding a suitable man was like searching for a needle in a haystack. Kamani was not into the club or bar scene, and finding someone in church was not cutting it; most of the single male members were as old as Methuselah or had more health-related problems than one could count. This is not to say she was hard to please, but most of the men she encountered in the past were married, gay or bisexual, and the men she did date were either afraid to commit or just wanted to be friends with benefits.

This is not what she wanted out of life; she was searching for a man who shared the same interests and values as she did. He did not have to be rich but had to be financially sound. Living with a man without the benefit of marriage was not an option for her.

During the fifth year of operation, sales from the company had tripled. Kamani was now ready to expand her business. She did not want to limit herself to just the Oakland area but possibly go nationwide. Someone suggested the Internet. The concept of going on-line was a new phenomenon for her. She did not even have an e-mail account because her business was local.

Most of Kamani's clients came to her office, or she would go to their place of business to discuss designing or printing needs. Nevertheless, after careful examination, she knew conducting business in cyberspace was the way to go if she were going to broaden her horizons and increase revenues. Her computer came with a modem and an Internet Service Provider program. She opened an e-mail account and signed on for complete access to the World Wide Web.

While surfing the Internet, she found several sites on which to advertise her company. Soon, she received many inquiries and signed on three clients from the Greater East Bay area. For the next several months, her ads were pulling in orders from as far away as Australia.

In her spare time, Kamani would go on-line to seek out other business opportunities and noticed rotating banners advertising dating sites. She was amazed that so many of these services were on-line. She would see ads for dating and matchmaking services in printed newspapers and singles' publications but never realized the Internet held so many possibilities for meeting someone. With numerous choices, she was baffled as to which sites to check.

She was like a kid in the candy store and thought, *If only I had known about these places years ago, I might have met a suitable mate right on the World Wide Web.* She made up her mind to start searching for love and romance and believed there was a reason why she went on-line in the first place: It was not to get more customers but to find a soul mate.

Kismet was working in Kamani's favor, she thought. After probing through a myriad of dating sites, she found a service, which targeted the forty plus singles. She put together a short profile and uploaded it along with her photo:

44-year-old single female is seeking a genuine, loving and caring single male who is interested in a committed relationship, leading to marriage. Age is unimportant. I operate a successful business, own my own home and enjoy shopping, attending yard sales and dinning out, just to name a few.   For more details, contact me.

For the next couple of weeks, Kamani was browsing through some of the men's profiles, but none of the ads appealed to her. She knew it would take time to find that out-of-the-ordinary man. After all, it had been years since she was in a serious relationship. Therefore, there was no rush to meet anyone.

However, deep in her heart, she knew the likelihood of a 44-year-old woman finding someone becomes harder as one gets older and believed that most men in this age group were looking for younger women who could bear them offsprings; at this stage of her life, she was not interested in having children.

Since her parents were deceased, and she had no siblings, Kamani had no family obligations. Because most of her relatives were scattered throughout the country, she had very little contact with them.

Kamani was a very attractive and petite woman, had a very youthful looking face and kept herself in good physical condition by walking and jogging. When it came to her sense of style, she was very conservative and was not into name-brand designer clothes or flashy trinkets. She was definitely penny-pinching chic.

Her home was modestly furnished and decorated. Most of the paintings on her walls were copies or prints. She enjoyed searching for bargains and taking advantage of sales and specials on office equipment and add-ons for the house. On the weekends, she loved shopping at the thrift shops and attending yard sales. To say she was a prudent person was no exaggeration. If she could buy anything below wholesale, she did.

Finally, Kamani received an e-mail with an attached photo from an interested suitor. His name was Landel. He came across her profile, was in awe of her beauty and described himself as a 50-year-old never-married man who was an executive at a bank in the Republic of Cape Verde.

His job was to set up and oversee business accounts for foreign corporations doing business in his country. One of his hopes and dreams was to meet a woman like her. He went on to write that he was a one-woman man who was also looking to marry, and her age was irrelevant. He enjoyed reading, traveling, listening to classical music and playing chess and the piano, was a loving and caring person and was seeking the same qualities in a woman. He was planning to visit California on business and wanted to meet her.

After reading that e-mail and looking at his picture, Kamani fell completely for this man. He was drop-dead gorgeous. She could not believe that such a refined and sexy looking, middle-aged man was out there. *Sometimes you have to go the distance to find someone so beautiful.*

For Kamani, it was love at first sight, and yet, she was about to be weaved into a web of make-believe, which would leave her devastated for years to come.

For the next two months, Landel and Kamani were e-mailing each other and chatting on-line. He would send sexy photos of himself, seductive notes and love verses from which she got great pleasure; in return, she would do the same.

Not only was Landel well bred but extremely romantic. She would have fantasies about the two of them embracing each other in front of the fireplace, sipping wine in the nude, chasing each other around the house, ending up on the futon and making passionate love all night. She could not believe that such sensual thoughts were racing through her head. This man really had a hold on her, and he definitely rocked her world.

Landel talked about his life growing up in Cape Verde and the businesses that were investing in his country. He even suggested that there was a market for her service. While he was talking more about commerce, she was thinking about expanding her business, reaching a wider market and starting a line of t-shirts, silk-screened with her artwork and designs. She came up with a proposal, sent it to him for feedback and asked for his assistance in setting up this type of undertaking in his homeland.

Within a couple of days, Landel got back to Kamani, thought her proposition was excellent and advised her that starting a corporation of this type, in Cape Verde, would be beneficial. People are always looking for uniquely designed t-shirts due to their popularity, and merchants are willing to pay big bucks for high-end tees.

He told her there was a plant in the city of Paria that could print and distribute her merchandise to various stores and outlets worldwide for next to nothing. All she would have to do is provide the artwork, and the factory would take care of the rest. She would have to open a corporate account at his bank. They could discuss this project in more details because he was planning to visit California next month.

By now, Kamani's impressions of Landel's intellect in international trade rated him a high mark; she could not stop thinking about how caring and encouraging he was in helping her reach her goals. Each day, she was falling in love with this man and could not wait to see him. His magnetic approach was quickly becoming her drug of choice and was pulling her deeper into a never-ending abyss.

While Kamani was on the Internet, she received an e-mail from Landel, informing her that the owner of the factory was looking to sell. The asking price was one million dollars, which included eight printing presses, t-shirts, dependable workers and a roster of buyers. She would only have to put down twenty percent as a good faith payment and with the intent to buy. He told her there were several people interested in acquiring the plant, and if she wanted to buy the factory, he would have to hear from her within forty-eight hours.

She was eager and immediately e-mailed him. *I want to purchase the plant and set up an account at your bank.*

He e-mailed her back and conveyed, *I will handle all of the particulars and get back to you shortly.*

Two days later, she received the following e-mail:

Dear Kamani:

The lawyer representing the factory you wish to buy has prepared a contract along with the necessary documents, which will transfer ownership of the business to you.

You agree to pay two hundred thousand dollars, {twenty percent deposit of the total asking price, one million dollars}, which will be deposited into the seller's bank account. You and the seller will determine subsequent payments of the remaining balance {eight hundred thousand dollars} later.

I will e-mail the contract to you shortly; please sign and return by fax as soon as possible. To expedite this agreement, I have taken the liberty of contacting a lawyer who is an associate of mine; he specializes in business contracts and will be in your area for the next several days.

At my request, he will go over the contract at no cost to you. Please note that ownership of the company will be complete when the seller receives two hundred thousand dollars into his account.
Love and Smooches,
Landel

In his business affairs, Kamani could not believe how professional Landel was. Here was a man who got things done. Unlike many of the men she encountered in the past, he was not afraid to make important decisions or stand by his promises. He walked the walk and talked the talk, was a take charge individual and was definitely the man she wanted to be with, without end.

The documents had arrived. Kamani read them thoroughly and thought the terms were clear but took Landel's advice and called the lawyer whom he had recommended. She made an appointment to see the legal representative. Since he was going to be in the vicinity, he agreed to come to her home office.

When the attorney arrived, they both went over the papers. He explained everything, informed her that the contract was thorough and wished her good fortunes. He was leaving the country in a couple of days and left his cell phone number in case she had any additional questions. She thanked him for his assistance.

Kamani signed and faxed the papers to Landel. The next day, he notified her that the documents had arrived, and after receiving the two hundred thousand dollars, she would receive the title to the plant. He gave her the seller's account number to wire the money into and told her it would take one month for the transaction to be completed. Once she got the deed, he would send an application, which would make it possible for her to open a corporate account.

On Friday morning, Kamani went to the bank and wired two hundred thousand dollars into the seller's bank account. She was in such high spirits; one would have thought she won the million-dollar lottery.

After arriving home, Kamani called her friends for a get-together at her place and told them she had great news to share. The gathering would take place next Friday evening at eight o'clock. She could not wait to brag about the new man in her life and their latest business venture.

It was Friday, and Kamani was on high octane. She prepared an elaborate buffet style dinner and had Sangria on ice. Her guests started to arrive; she greeted everyone with an immense hug and kiss. They all sat around, talked and were eager to hear what she had to say.

After dinner, everyone was patiently waiting for her to talk. Finally, Kamani revealed how she met and fell in love with a man named Landel, and he lived in Cape Verde. He helped her to purchase a factory that would print and distribute her designer t-shirts globally. She went on to discuss every aspect about the business, from start to finish, and this all took place on the World Wide Web.

For the very first time, her friends were speechless. Most of them never even heard of Cape Verde, much less knew where it was. It was not a place written about or mentioned repeatedly in the media. They started to question among themselves, "How does an educated woman fall in love with a stranger and then buy a business from someone she met on the Internet?"

Continuing to talk uncontrollably, Kamani felt like the main character in a soap opera and the center of attention for a change.

It did not take long for her friends to realize that Landel had swindled Kamani out of her money. Yet, no one had the heart to tell her; if they did, she would have become very defensive, because the love of her life would never deceive her in such a way. No matter what anyone thought, she made the right decision, end of story.

Later that evening, her party started to leave and thanked her for an enlightening evening. They all wished her well but knew the damage had already taken place. It was just a matter of time before Kamani's world would come crashing down on her like a ton of bricks. All the same, her friends would be there to help pick up the pieces.

Six weeks went by, and Kamani had not heard from Landel regarding the title to the factory. She e-mailed him every day and still there was no word. At first, she thought he was traveling on business and planning to come to

California. She decided to call the lawyer to see if he had seen or heard from Landel, but the number was not in service. She had to leave the office for a couple of hours to deliver a job to one of her customers.

When Kamani got back home, there were several messages on her answering machine; she thought one of the calls was from Landel, but they were all from business associates and concerned friends. She went on her computer to check her e-mail but heard nothing from him. She sent another fax and still there was no reply.

She went back on-line to do a search on the bank. Its headquarters' address, e-mail and telephone number came up. She called the bank and after further investigation discovered that Landel never worked at the bank but had an account there.

When she inquired about the money wired into the seller's account, the bank manager said, "The money went into Landel's account. Two weeks after receiving the funds, he withdrew the money and closed the account."

After hearing that shocking information, Kamani dropped the phone, became dizzy, fell to the floor and screamed. She could not deem the man she fell in love with would have the inclination to put together such an evil scheme. He came over as such an honorable man.

How could an individual who sent her love letters and romantic poems transform himself into such a diabolical character? He was a chameleon who fooled her into thinking he was a person with a heart but under that pretense was a wicked impostor. She felt abused and exploited, because this man stripped away her dignity.

Just about everyone in the community heard about Kamani's troubles. Many wondered how a bright and successful business-minded woman became the victim of fraud so effortlessly. Rumors started to spread that she was financially ruined and was about to lose her business and home. The chatter was somewhat true. She was at the brink of losing everything.

By chance, Kamani was able to refinance her home and obtain an additional line of credit. Yet, the money she lost did not pain her as much as Landel's deception. She contemplated pressing charges against him but knew it was fruitless. She never even met the man and had no idea if he really lived in Cape Verde.

She started to speculate that the photo he sent of himself was probably a fake, and he might have been pretending to be the seller and the lawyer, or maybe all three of them were in on the con.

Law enforcement could not assist her because the ruse occurred outside of the United States. Once you have delved into a foreign affair, the laws do not protect you.

One could say, "She was dealing with the phantom of the Internet," because there were no legal recourses to get her money back. It was gone forever, but the ache of the duplicity would become etched in her heart and soul without end.

Kamani decided to take some time off from the business. She contacted all of her clients, reassured them that she was still in business and would return in two weeks. If they needed a rush job, she would give them the name of an associate, but her patrons were very loyal and would wait for her until she got back.

While on retreat, she thought about the blunders she made throughout her life when it came to selecting men. As she became older, she thought she was wiser, but apparently, this was not the case. She reflected on the bitterness she had towards her married friends but overlooked an important cautionary sign: Landel was too good to be true.

Her haste to find a man clouded her judgment and cost her dearly, but she believed bad occurrences do happen for a reason and learned a very valuable lesson from this disastrous occurrence. She would never trust men again, swore them off for good and discovered that being alone was not the end of the world.

When Kamani returned home, there were many messages on her voice mail. It would take her almost three days to get back to all the callers. She went on-line to check her e-mail. There must have been over one hundred messages in her box; most were orders and advertisements, but one particular message caught her eye. It was from a man responding to her personal profile:

Hi:

I was browsing through the dating site and came across your ad. You are a beautiful woman and reading your profile lifted my spirits, because I just came out of a long-term relationship and never thought I would find someone like you.

You sound so gentle, and this is why I contacted you. We have a lot in common. My name is Joneh, and I am 46 years old, never been married and have no children. I own my home and a Laundromat in the Chicago area. I enjoy dinning out, attending plays and reading romance novels. I would love to get to know you more.

Looking forward to hearing from you. Goodbye.

After reading that e-mail, Kamani did not know whether to laugh or cry but knew she had to do two things: Delete the message and cancel her membership.♦

Seduction and Love In Cyberspace

Nia felt her life was as mundane as an inanimate object. Yet, lifeless items can be functional and add beauty to any environment. She looked at life differently from the rest of the world. Never mind, she held a high paying position as a stockbroker at one of the most prestigious brokerage firms in New York City, was making a six figure income and owned a condominium in an upscale neighborhood that was quickly becoming the place to be for the up and coming Who's Who in America.

She had a growing list of wealthy clients who were looking to invest their money to make more, and this was her forte, making the rich, richer. At age 28, she was one of the top stockbrokers at her company, earned high commissions and huge bonuses. She had a supportive family, a large circle of friends and associates, entertained often and dated on a regular basis.

Yet, most of the men Nia met were either conservative or egotistical. For some reason, she was attracting men who did not add any excitement to her life. No matter how much education, money or status the men possessed, she found these guys to be as dull as she was and sensed something was definitely missing in her life, and it was time for her to do a complete change.

Many of Nia's acquaintances would discuss how they found their ideal love on the Internet. She held the firm belief that going on the World Wide Web to find a mate was a sign of desperation but thought, if her associates were using this type of venue to find romance then maybe this could be something worth checking.

So, one night, against her better judgment, she went on-line to browse through some of the more popular dating sites. One particular service caught her eye. Since joining was free, she had nothing to lose; she registered and then became a premium member. She carefully scripted her profile and submitted it along with her photo.

Since Nia was not one to sit back and wait for others to contact her, she started to surf the site for single men. Some of the profiles did not impress her. She felt that many of the men were not forthcoming in their description, income, status or relationship wishes.

After several weeks of searching, she was about to give up; suddenly, one particular profile captured her attention. What attracted her to this personal ad was that the man was strikingly handsome and came across as a sophisticated individual.

His name was Toto. He described himself as a never married, childless and God-fearing middle-aged man of means who was searching for the ideal woman with whom he could share his love and possessions. He was tall, muscular, physically fit, did not smoke or drink and was drug and disease-free. He owned an import-export business, came from a family of landowners and was seeking a woman who was financially independent and who wanted to have children in the near future.

The fact that he lived in Gabon might have been a drawback, but he enchanted Nia. All she saw was a good-looking man who measured up to her standards. She contacted him promptly, and for the next several months, they were e-mailing each other.

As a stockbroker, Nia's job was to help individual investors and large institutions increase their net worth. She wanted to do the same for Toto and invest his money into international stocks, bonds, commodities and mutual funds.

Toto believed he had found his love companion and business partner for life, too. Her financial expertise left a lasting impression on him, and he was ready to settle down. He proposed to her by e-mail and invited her to come to Gabon to be with him, even though the two never met in person. Their communication was through e-mail and snail mail. Eventually, they talked on the telephone, but every time he called, he would reverse the charges.

All the same, Nia accepted his marriage proposal and was happy as a cat that just snagged a mouse, because together they would be a wealthy and an influential couple.

Now that her life was in full swing, Nia told everyone that she had finally met her better half in cyberspace and intended to marry him. For the next twelve months, she was planning to relocate to Gabon. She quit her job, rolled over the money from her 401(k) plan into an IRA account, sold her condominium and placed all of her furnishings in storage until she was ready to send for them. She then moved all of her money into Toto's personal bank account.

People who knew Nia were bewildered to hear such news. Many started to wonder if she had completely lost her mind. Why would anyone, who had so much going for herself, take such drastic steps and put her career and finances in jeopardy?

Not born with a silver spoon in her mouth, she had to work hard to get where she was today, and to have thrown it all away did not make any sense, but it was logical to Nia, because all of her dreams had finally come true, but her visions were about to become her worst nightmare.

It took another six months for Nia to get all of her business in order. She was now set to leave the United States and take that long awaited trip to meet and marry her prince. She allowed herself enough money to get by on until she got to the city of Libreville, the capital of Gabon. At the end of the year, she booked a flight for a Friday morning departure from JFK International Airport and arrived in Libreville late that evening.

At the airport, Toto was anxiously waiting. When Nia first saw him, his physique surprised her. Instead of being tall and muscular, he was short and stocky, but his size was no longer an issue. All she cared about was meeting her prospective husband. The fact that he owned land and had money made him look first-rate in her eyes.

They embraced as though they had not seen each other in years.

He asked her how the flight went.

"It was a pleasant and long awaited journey," she responded.

"I am delighted to meet you," Toto said.

Nia was beautiful, tall and voluptuous and always wore her hair in tiny braids. She was a natural beauty, and her fashion style was always classic chic. She could have been a high fashion or a cover-girl model. As far as Toto was concerned, she was just what the doctor ordered.

The two left the airport in a taxi and arrived at Toto's residence in less than ten minutes. He lived in a small room, which hardly had any furnishings. The place had a bed, table, two chairs, a refrigerator and a stove.

The village, in which he resided, was such a contrast to where Nia had lived in New York. She started to wonder why an affluent person would live such a penny-pinching existence but rationalized that many wealthy people do live below their means; this is why they have money.

As Nia looked around the room, she asked Toto why he lived in a space with just the bare necessities. He told her his business had failed, and he had to sell all of his assets to pay off bad debts, which had accumulated over the past two years. Currently, he could only afford a one-room dwelling.

At that moment, Nia asked about the land his parents owned. "You could have used it as collateral or sold some of the land to pay down your debts," she stressed with a stunned look.

228

He said his uncle owned the land and not his parents. The family had been feuding for years, regarding the true ownership of the acreage. His uncle's father was the original owner, but when the father passed away, there were no provisions made as to which family member would take over the estate. Therefore, the uncle made a claim as the true owner.

She then asked him about her money.

"My beloved Nia, I took the liberty of using the money you sent to pay off all of my debts. I am sorry to say that I am broke with no means of paying you back right now."

At that moment, Nia stopped listening to him. Her head started to spin like a steering wheel out of control. After getting over that initial shock, she realized how a smooth operator had taken her for a ride. The money, which she worked so hard for was gone. If she thought her life was boring before she met Toto, Nia was in for a rude awakening, because she was now broke, and to make a bad situation worse, he still wanted to marry her.

Toto believed that with Nia's help, he could restart his business and make up for the money lost and said, "My family will help us get back on our feet."

As Nia started to evaluate her circumstances, she knew there was no future with Toto. She did not want to stay with him any longer. What would be the point? Both of them were insolvent. She had no money to take care of herself, much less take care of two people.

The cost of buying a one-way ticket back to the United States cost more than Nia could afford. She had no home to go back to, because she sold her condominium. All the same, she was fortunate in one way: She had family and friends who would be there for her and decided it was time to leave Toto's place.

Nia checked into an inexpensive motel, called her parents, explained her state of affairs and asked to have money for a plane ticket wired to her. Two days later, she left Gabon.

On the flight back to New York, Nia pondered how a man she hardly knew and never even met could have tricked her so easily. In retrospect, she started to ask herself why she did not recognize the hidden codes, which forewarned her that Toto was not forthcoming about himself. So many questions and thoughts were racing through her head.

When Toto described himself as a man of means, what exactly did he mean? Why did Toto always reverse the charges when he called me? Why did he not make an effort to come to the United States to meet me? When Toto asked me to marry him and invited me to come to Gabon, why did he not send me money for a plane ticket?

She knew it was pointless to ask these questions now. It was like putting the carriage in front of the horse. Nia came to terms with the poor choices she made in the name of love and learned a very valuable lesson.

As the plane landed at JFK International Airport, Nia started to recognize that her life was not as boring as she imagined. The road she traveled to search for love and to add more excitement to her so-called uninspiring life was a prelude to an elaborate deception carried out by Toto, with Nia being the injured party. Only time will tell if she will be able to pick up the pieces after a man whom she fell in love with and trusted so deeply misled her.

After getting off the plane, Nia retrieved her luggage. Waiting at the arrival gate were her parents. She hugged them, and the three drove off to her parents' home. She did not have the strength to carry on a conversation with them; she was quiet and too embarrassed to discuss what had taken place overseas. There would be plenty of time for that conversation. Now, Nia had more time than she had money.

Her mother inquired as to how her flight went.

"It was okay," she replied.

Her father, who was never at a loss for words, was silent throughout the ride.

It seemed as though it took forever for the family to arrive home. The trip from the airport usually took about fifteen minutes. After arriving home, Nia thanked her parents for being there. Her mother had prepared her daughter's bedroom.

Exhausted from the long flight, Nia decided to take a shower, went straight to bed and relentlessly thought about Toto's dishonesty. The replay of those events kept rotating in her head until she finally fell asleep.

It was morning, and Nia heard a knock at her bedroom door. It was her mother asking if she wanted to come down for breakfast, but she knew what her parents really wanted to do; they wanted to discuss what occurred in Gabon.

Since Nia never really went into any details about Toto, she was perplexed as to what she was going to say to them. All her parents knew was that their daughter had met a rich businessperson who lived in a foreign country, and she was going to marry him.

Nia was very close to her parents who worked hard to obtain the American dream. Her mother was a dressmaker and worked from home, and her father was a bookkeeper at a department store. On the side, he prepared income taxes. He was a frugal person and was not one to waste money on frivolous things. Every penny he earned went into a bank account.

When Nia's father accumulated enough money, he purchased a home for his family and sent both of his children to college. Nia majored in finance and her brother majored in biochemistry.

The son was a scientist at a pharmaceutical company and resided in Colorado with his wife and four children.

Nia's father was very proud of his adult children, because he saw a little bit of himself in them. He always taught them the value of a dollar, stressed that money did not grow on trees and if managed wisely, one could be self-sufficient and live a comfortable existence. His motto was, "A person should live below his or her means, and always save for a rainy day."

So, when his daughter sent all of her money to Gabon and subsequently lost it all, he was shocked and started to wonder if his daughter was under some kind of hypnotic spell while she was communicating with this man. *Perhaps Toto was sprinkling goofa dust on the letters he was sending to her.*

The aroma from the bacon and eggs, waffles and coffee was so tempting. Nia could not resist joining her parents for breakfast. Inhaling a mouthful of fresh air before going downstairs, she was not looking forward to facing her parents. She figured now would be a good time to explain what happened but would leave out most of the facts.

As Nia sat down at the table, she started to tell her parents what had taken place but never told them how Toto had used all of her money to pay off his debts.

She said, "Toto and I had invested all of our money into a business venture, which was a sure winner, but the deal fell through when one of the investors had disappeared with all of the money." She just could not bring herself to tell them that her fiancé was the culprit.

Her father, being a perceptive man, did not buy her story. His daughter was a bright money manager. She would have never put all of her eggs into one basket. Her mother just sat there in amazement and did not know what to think or say. Nevertheless, her parents decided not to push the subject any further and concluded: If their daughter wanted them to know more, she would have told them.

After breakfast, Nia went back to her bedroom and contemplated her next move. She knew staying with her mom and dad was not an option, because having her own space was an indication of being independent. Without delay, she contacted some of her business associates and friends. Because of her excellent negotiating skills, she would have no problems finding a job.

In no time, Nia got a position as a financial consultant at a bank in mid-town Manhattan. The starting salary was sixty-five thousand dollars. For her, it was like starting all over.

The company did offer good benefits, which included complete health care coverage, a pension plan, bonuses, paid holidays, sick leave, paid personal days and two weeks paid vacation after one year of employment. She would work in the Mutual Funds Division. Her job was to get customers with large accounts to invest their money into these funds.

In her new job, Nia was right at home. Her reputation was well known. Everyone at the bank knew of her achievements at the brokerage firm but asked why she left such a lucrative position to come work for a bank.

She would just say, "The mounting pressures of working for a large investment institution were just too much. I needed more balance in my life and decided to leave the company, do some traveling and find a position that was less demanding." That was it. She learned not to broadcast all of personal business to her co-workers.

It was now the first anniversary of Nia's employment. She accrued quite a bit of money and decided it was time to look for a place of her own. She found an affordable one-bedroom apartment not too far from work, signed a two-year lease and moved in. Bit by bit, she added furniture, decorative ornaments and works of art to make the place more relaxing and welcoming.

Between working at the bank and decorating the apartment, Nia was busy and had very little time to date or entertain. She often thought about Toto and wondered if he was back to posting his profile on the dating site.

She decided it was time to get back into the dating scene and went on-line to check out some sites but was determined not to make the same mistakes as she did with Toto. If she did meet someone on the Internet, she would not jump into a relationship so hastily.

Nia joined another dating service and uploaded her profile and photo. This time, she was going to wait and let the person of interest contact her.

Several days later, Nia received an e-mail with an attached photo from a man living in Dallas, Texas. His message was very enchanting.

He was a 36-year-old physically fit single male who was seeking a motivated, smart and independent single woman for a relationship leading to marriage. He operated a real estate investment company, owned his own home and traveled often. He received his MBA Degree from an esteemed university in Boston, dabbled in on-line trading and made some money buying and selling stocks. He was impressed with her profile and striking beauty.

Because he felt they both had so much in common, he wanted to form an on-line friendship and eventually meet her in person. His name was Dan.

After reading Dan's e-mail, Nia thought long and hard before answering him. She did not want to come over as being anxious and made a decision to wait a little longer before contacting him. If he did not respond, he was just looking for a roll in the hay or simply playing her. She waited four weeks before answering him.

In no time, Dan contacted her, and for the next several months, they were exchanging e-mails and letters. She admired him, because he did not pressure her into meeting or forming any type of personal connection.

Dan was all business and talked mostly about his real estate investment company. He would buy dilapidated houses, renovate and re-sell them and make a nice profit. He sent photos of the refurbished homes to Nia. The houses were so beautiful that she was thinking of purchasing one as an investment.

After communicating for almost a year, Dan informed Nia that he was coming to New York on business and wanted to meet her. She was more than confident in getting-together with him and mentioned some great hotels and guesthouses where he could stay. In two weeks, he would arrive in New York. So excited, she could not wait to see him and believed he was the one.

Dan arrived in New York. He was staying at a hotel, which was not too far from Nia's apartment. He called and arranged to meet her for dinner at a restaurant near the hotel. Changing outfits several times, she felt like a teenager going out on her first date and settled on a red satin off the shoulder dress and a black knit jacket. Looking in the mirror, she said, "You go girl" and was on her way to meeting her date.

When Nia arrived at the restaurant, she saw Dan. He looked just like his photo. He was tall, dark and handsome and came over as a stylish person. When Dan saw Nia, he got up, hugged her and said how delighted he was to meet her, and her picture did not do her justice.

"You are more stunning in person," he said.

She started to blush. Fascinated by his charming demeanor, she said, "Thank you, Dan."

Throughout dinner, Dan and Nia talked about their interests and dreams for the future. He was definitely paying attention to her as she was to him. They appeared to be star struck lovers stranded on an island and trying to determine what to do next.

After dinner, the two went back to her place for a nightcap. When they arrived at her residence, he was amazed and said, "Your apartment is lovely."

She thanked him and offered him a drink. They continued to talk. With his help, she wanted to buy a house in Texas.

"I would be delighted to help you find a home that would fit into your budget. I have a couple of properties that are ready to go on the market," Dan said.

Nia could not take time off from her job, because she had already used up her vacation time. It would be another year before she could travel and did not want to miss a great opportunity since it was a buyer's market.

Dan told her that she did not have to come to Texas; he would send her a video of the finished homes. If she were interested in making a bid, he could handle all of the paper work from his end. She would have to put down a ten percent deposit, and he would hold the mortgage for her.

The houses cost anywhere from three hundred thousand dollars to five hundred thousand dollars. A one family split-level home with two bedrooms and two baths was approximately three hundred thousand dollars. She thought the price was right and would utilize the house as a rental property. Being so overjoyed, she asked him to spend the night. The two engaged in hot and erotic lovemaking for over four hours. It was a night she would never fail to forget.

The next morning, Nia woke up on top of the world. Dan was still asleep. She got up and took a shower. As she was coming out of the bathroom, he had awakened. They greeted each other with a deep tender kiss and got dressed.

She went to the kitchen and made breakfast. They sat down and talked about the previous night and how awesome it was. Dan was going to remain in New York for another week. The two had a whirlwind romance and took in some sightseeing and shopping.

On the last day of Dan's visit, he went back to the hotel, checked out and returned to Nia's apartment. She made up her mind then; he was going to be her significant other. The two made fiery love until dawn. It was now time for him to get up and depart for his trip back to Dallas. As he was leaving, he whispered, "I love you."

"I am in love with you and want to take our relationship to the next level," Nia said.

He left her place and hailed a cab to the airport.

If Nia thought her dreams of love and ecstasy were about to come true, she was in for the biggest revelation of her being.

A week later, Dan sent her a video and photos of three finished homes. She fell in love with the first house, which was located twenty miles north of Dallas. She agreed to the ten percent down payment, got a loan from a private lending company and sent a cashier's check for thirty thousand dollars to Dan's Real Estate Investment Company.

A month had gone by, and Nia had not heard from Dan. For the next several days, she e-mailed him but never got a reply. She called his company but kept getting his voice mail. She thought it was time to go to Texas and was able to take some personal days.

Nia made flight reservations to leave Friday morning, arrived in Texas in the afternoon and took a cab to Dan's company, which turned out to be a mail drop service.

When Nia inquired about Dan's Real Estate Investment Company, the clerk informed her that the company had closed its box, and no forwarding address was on file.

It did not take a rocket scientist to guess what had occurred. She was taken in again and started to wonder, *What was it about me that attracted these underhanded men into my life, and what signals did I release that would cause me to be deceived not once but twice?*

After Toto's betrayal, she thought for sure she was more levelheaded and astute to reading people. Filing a complaint against Dan or trying to get her money back was useless. For all she knew, Dan was not his real name. He was probably in another state or country, under an assumed name, back on the Internet and attempting to defraud another poor soul out of her money.

She was able to get a flight out that evening. On her way back home, she made a mental note to herself: *There will be no more searching for romance on the World Wide Web, and I can be miserable by myself.*♦

Cyberspace Vixen

You could say Jamo was born with a silver spoon in his mouth. His parents owned and operated a car dealership for over 30 years in the Washington, D.C. community; they were approaching retirement age and grooming him, their only child, to take over the company. Yet, he had other ideas and no interest in the business. When his parents left him in charge, he knew how to worm his way out of an assignment by getting other employees to do his work. He was as slippery as a wet eel.

Jamo's paternal grandparents, who were now deceased, had set up a trust fund, which he could not draw from until he was twenty-six years old. They believed at this age, their grandson would be more mature at managing and investing his money sensibly.

He did receive a small monthly allowance from his parents. When he got all of his money from the trust, he would fly the coop, travel the world and live a jet set lifestyle. He had it all worked out and was slowly planning his departure.

For several years, Jamo had been attending college, but his major was a complete mystery to those who knew him. He was attending college, because his parents stipulated that in order to receive his monthly pocket money, he had to either work at the dealership full-time or attend college. He chose the latter. However, his parents never gave him a timetable to obtain his degree, so going to school became his vocation.

There were times when he would cut classes, get students to take notes for him or pay to have his assignments and term papers done. He was extremely good at manipulating people and talking his way out of any situation. His mannerism and charm were his greatest assets. Women would gravitate towards him like groupies encircling a pop star; they would do just about anything for and to him.

The talk around campus was that many women and a few good men would offer Jamo money to spend the night with them, and some professors would give him a passing grade for courses, which he never completed or passed, for a night of erotic indulgences. Whether these rumors were true, no one really knew. Others would just hang around him because of the big windfall that was coming his way.

Frankly speaking, no one could have ever blamed these people for wanting to be into him. After all, he was drop-dead attractive, had the body of an Olympic runner and spent more time in the gym than he did in the lecture halls. His sense of style was laid-back. With his long beautiful locs, he kept up with the latest fashion trends. No matter what he wore, heads would turn.

In three months, Jamo would reach twenty-six. In the meantime, he started to go on-line to plan his journey but could not decide which country to visit first. He thought about going to St. Kitts, the birthplace of his grandparents who came to the United States in the 1940s. When he was a little boy, they always talked about how beautiful and rich in history the island was, and he should go there, someday, to meet the other side of the family and maybe set up permanent roots.

Jamo's parents would travel back and forth to the island to check on their other businesses: A bread and breakfast inn and a high-end clothing store. They were preparing to return there to live out their retirement years.

He quickly scratched that idea and wanted to get as far away from his parents as possible. This is not to say he did not love or appreciate them, but his mother and father were always placing demands on him when it came to running and taking over the dealership. He tried to make it clear to them: He wanted no part of the business.

If left up to him, Jamo would sell the dealership, but his parents would not hear of it and could not comprehend what he was trying to convey to them. All of the other workers at the company got the message about his lack of interest in the establishment. Why his parents could not recognize this was the sixty-four thousand dollar question. He went back to surfing the Internet.

It was now summer break, and most of the women Jamo was seeing left town. Since he was not planning to return to college and was leaving D.C., he would never see any of his schoolmates or friends again. He was starting to feel restless and lonely. After all, he was never without a female at his side. His cell phone had numbers of college women of every age, size, shape and color, and if he had the inclination, he could have started a dating, modeling, or an escort service.

During the summer, Jamo had no choice but to work at the dealership full-time, but in two months, he would reach twenty-six. For him, it would be goodbye car dealership, hello to all that money, and a bright new future. He continued to do as little work as possible. When his parents were not there, he would spend time on the Internet instead of attending to the customers.

While on-line, he checked out some of the dating sites and laughed at a few of the men's profiles, because he never had to go on-line to find a woman. He was a suave and sophisticated young gent. All he had to do was stroll down the street, and women would approach him without any hesitation and believed he would have the same outcome in cyberspace.

Proving that he had the power to draw in women, Jamo elected to place his profile on the site. After writing and perfecting his personal ad, he uploaded it along with a snapshot of himself. His posting read as follows:

My name is Jamo, and I am single. As you can see from my picture, I am a handsome and well-groomed male. My aspiration is to meet a classy single female who enjoys going out and attending social functions. I attend a prominent university in Washington, D.C. and am currently working at my parents' car dealership. My interests are traveling and meeting new people in far away places. In two months, I will turn twenty-six, come into a large sum of money and plan to live abroad. If you would like to know more about me, send an e-mail along with your photo.

Jamo was quite proud of his ad and knew he would receive loads of responses.

What woman in her right mind would not take immediate action to my personal ad? His photo alone was enough to make women, young and old, fall to their knees and be at his disposal.

Regrettably, his ego was about to get the best of him. A cyberspace vixen was plotting to weave him into a web of lies and deception. If Jamo thought he was the great manipulator, he was dead wrong. He was about to meet his counterpart, and she would commit one of the most unspeakable acts that would make a man tough as nails breakdown and weep.

It had been a couple of weeks since Jamo was on-line. His parents had him coming and going at the company. Some of the salespeople were on vacation, so he could not get out of doing any work. By the end of the day, he was exhausted. He was counting the days to draw on his trust fund and leaving this humdrum way of life forever.

Jamo had taken a couple of days off from work. He told his parents he was not feeling well and could do some of the paper work from home. Of course, this was not true. He had other fish to fry and went on-line to check his e-mail.

There must have been over three hundred responses to his personal ad. He started to read some of the replies. Most of them went into the trash bin and others to the maybe folder, but one e-mail caught his attention because it had an attached video. When he downloaded the clip, it started to play:

"Permit me to inform you of my desire to meet you. I came across your personal profile along with your stunning picture and started to have feelings, which I have never experienced in my life, and this is why I decided to get in touch with you. I cannot imagine how you must feel receiving my video from a far away place. My name is Malana; I am 24, 5'8" tall and single. I live in Benin and speak French and English. I received my Degree in Banking and Finance. I enjoy going out and meeting people of different cultures, have traveled extensively and plan to visit America shortly. My interests are reading, jogging, listening to music, cooking and going to museums and plays. I sense a strong connection to you and want to get to know you better. Please tell me more about yourself, your likes and dislikes, family, country, etc. I believe we can develop a connection that might direct us to be together. I wish to let you know that sincerity is very important to me, even though we might be thousands of miles away from each other. If you would like to know more about me, please contact me soon."

Malana's video grabbed Jamo's attention. Her voice was beyond sexy. She was a work of art. Her flawless skin gleamed like the Great Blue diamond, and her hair was styled in cornrows with extended braids. She wore a short burgundy dress, and her deep chocolate eyes had an air of secrecy. To say she was a goddess was no exaggeration.

For Jamo, it was love at first sight. He played that clip several times. No woman has ever had a hold like this on him. He was the love them and leave them type of person. He quickly deleted the remaining messages and contacted her.

For the next several weeks, Jamo and Malana were corresponding by e-mail. She wrote about her life growing up in Benin, the number of countries she had visited, and her job as a financial analyst for large banks and financial institutions. She had her own apartment and mentioned how one could live quite comfortably on very little money in her country. This bit of information was of interest to Jamo since he was planning to relocate anyway. Perhaps, Benin could be that place.

He told her he would be receiving a large sum of money soon, and maybe he could travel to Benin for an extended vacation. She was planning to visit D.C. in a week or two and wanted to meet and spend some time with him.

Since Jamo was still living at home with his parents, he could not invite Malana to stay with him and would not tell them about her until he was ready to leave D.C. He e-mailed her and recommended a nice inn within walking distance from the university campus. She responded, gave him her arrival date, made reservations at the hotel and was due to arrive on a Friday afternoon, two days before Jamo's birthday.

For the next two weeks, Jamo was in high spirits. The staff noticed a complete change in him. He was actually working; he never got anyone to take over his sales. Some thought he was finally coming around to taking over the company. Since he was coming into money, he would either expand the business or open a second auto dealership in another locale. Whatever the reasons were, the staff was pleased; he was finally earning his stipend.

Today, Malana was due to arrive. Jamo left work to meet her at the airport and arrived about thirty minutes before the plane was due to land. While sitting and waiting, he was contemplating on what he was going to say to her. He was never off course for words when it came to women. So why was he so nervous now? He was like a teen going out on his first date and did not know what to expect.

The plane from Benin arrived on time. As Jamo approached the arrival gate, he saw Malana. His knees started to buckle. The video did not do her justice. She was more striking in person. When she saw Jamo, she had a smile that would have made a raging bull become docile. Getting closer, she embraced him and said, "I have waited all my life to meet someone like you, and I am thrilled to be here; you are my destiny."

He quickly replied, "The feeling is mutual. How was your flight?"

"There was much turbulence, but I kept gazing at your photo, and my fears had completely vanished."

If Jamo had any qualms about what he was going to say, her words squashed those doubts. When the two got into a taxi, he never stopped talking until they got to the inn.

After arriving at the hotel, Malana checked in. The hotel attendant escorted both of them to her suite. She was tired from the long flight and told Jamo she wanted to unpack, take a shower and rest for about one hour.

Jamo told her he would leave and come back, and they could have dinner in the hotel or at a local restaurant. Malana wanted to have dinner in her room and asked him to join her. He would return in two hours.

Jamo went home to freshen up but could not decide what to wear. He looked into his closet, which had more clothes than a men's fashion warehouse. After trying on several outfits, he decided on a navy blue suit, a light blue shirt and a red tie. He definitely wanted to make a good impression.

Well-rested, Malana was ready to set her scheme into action. She sprayed her body with jasmine scent and opted to wear a sexy red bustier, hip hugging black leather pants and red stilettos. For dinner, she ordered tossed salad with French dressing, baked oysters topped with garlic sauce, steamed asparagus, toasted baguette and a chilled bottle of sparkling wine. Dessert was chocolate covered strawberries dipped in whipped cream.

Jamo had arrived at the hotel; the clerk at the desk rang Malana to inform her that her guest had arrived and was on his way. When Jamo got to her room, he knocked on the door. As she opened the door, for a split second, he thought he had died and gone to heaven and actually had a euphoric episode.

She kissed him and escorted him into the suite where dinner was waiting.

He quickly came back to earth and made a comment about her attire, which unquestionably turned him on; he was now under her command.

Malana did most of the talking. When Jamo mentioned that in two days he would receive one million dollars from his trust fund, she came up with ways to invest his money and make it grow. He could come to Benin, live there for a while and get a feel for the place. She explained, "You can set up a brokerage account and transfer your money into any bank. Once an account is established, you can have a set amount of money wired to you, no matter where you live."

Jamo thought this was an excellent plan. Malana had asked him to spend the night. He did, and it was a night he would always remember. The two made intense love until they fell asleep.

When Jamo woke up Saturday morning, he was re-energized. He had fallen hard for Malana and did not want to leave. He called his parents to let them know he would be home in the evening. The two made zealous love again until mid-afternoon. They ordered lunch, talked about Jamo's money strategies and resumed to make non-stop love into the early evening.

He was now deeply in love with her. There was no doubt about it. He was going to spend the rest of his life with this woman. The excitement she felt was just too overpowering. If he tried, he could not resist her. She was now his aphrodisiac. He certainly did not need that popular blue pill to keep him coming and going. If she had told him to jump into the Potomac River, blindfolded and naked, he would have gladly obeyed her.

The two decided to go out to dinner. Jamo went home to change and told his parents he would be home very late. They reminded him not to make any plans for Sunday evening. He assured them he would not.

In front of the campus, Malana and Jamo dined at an intimate restaurant. He explained that he attended that institution but did not plan to get his degree; he was going to school to placate his parents and to receive his monthly cash. Starting Sunday, he would be on his own and make all decisions without any interference from them.

Jamo continued to ramble like a broken parakeet, but Malana maneuvered the conversation back to his trust fund and informed him that she was only going to be in D.C. for a week. She advised him that since the trust fund was already at the local bank, he could open a personal account and move the money there.

"When you're ready to go to the bank, I'll accompany you," she said.

He would go to the bank Monday morning and follow her recommendations. She invited him back to her room and once again, they made red-hot love until two in the morning.

It was three o'clock, Sunday morning when Jamo got home. Malana had worn him out. As his head hit the pillow, he instantly fell asleep. When his eyes opened, he got out of bed, took a shower and dressed. It was now 6:00 p.m.

Jamo wondered what his parents were planning for him. It was silent throughout the house. When he went downstairs and walked into the living room, everyone shouted "Surprise!" and started to sing *Happy Birthday*.

He was delighted. Employees, customers and business associates were there for the celebration; they congratulated him on reaching his twenty-sixth birthday and wished him many more years of good health and prosperity. He was in high spirits but sad at the same time, because Malana was not there. It did not matter, because he was going to be spending the rest of his life with her.

It was near midnight, and the guests were starting to leave. Jamo expressed his gratitude to everyone for coming and thanked his parents for putting together such a lovely birthday party.

"What are you going to do with your money?" his parents asked.

"Invest it wisely," he replied.

They smiled, nodded with approval and said, "Your grandparents would be very proud of you if they were here. You were their only grandchild, and they wanted to make certain that you were provided with all the means necessary to live a good and productive life."

Jamo's grandparents were born in St. Kitts and owned several successful businesses. When they came to America, their goal was to open a real estate agency, and they did. Their son, Jamo's father, who grew up in the sixties, obtain his Degree in Business Administration. While in college, he met his wife, who came from a very prominent family in the Baltimore area. The couple ended up working in the real estate business.

After the death of Jamo's grandparents, his parents inherited the real estate company but sold it, and with the proceeds from the sale, they started a car dealership that grew into a very successful enterprise.

"In two years, we will retire, return to St. Kitts and expect you to take over the business."

Jamo sat there, unenthusiastically, grinning like a Cheshire cat.

It was near 1:00 a.m. His parents turned in for the night; he went to his room and called Malana. They chatted for about two hours. He would meet her at the hotel in several hours and go straight to the bank.

It was almost 9:00 a.m., and Jamo was ready to leave. His parents wanted to know if he was joining them for breakfast; he said no and told them he was taking the day off to take care of some personal business.

He met Malana, and they went to the bank. He spoke to the bank manager and requested to have his money moved into a personal account. The manager suggested opening a brokerage account, but Malana quickly interrupted and said, "He will need more time to think about that. Being his financial advisor, I will make recommendations on the best brokerage firms."

The manager, sitting there with a stunned look on his face, was attempting to determine who this woman was. *When did this woman become Jamo's mouthpiece?* After all, the administrator knew the family for many years, and the money from the trust would remain at the bank. If the bank manager showed signs of confusion, it would not be long before the rest of the community would be befuddled.

One million dollars went into Jamo's private account. Jamo and Malana thanked the manager, left the bank and went back to the hotel. The two celebrated by toasting each other with champagne; she reminded him to open an on-line bank account. "It is more convenient and easier to transfer funds without having to go to the bank," she emphasized.

They then went to bed and made love for the remaining day. While in bed, he asked her to marry him. She accepted his proposal with steadfast delight and said, "I will be sending you information on some great brokerage companies. Do nothing with the money until you hear from me."

"Yes, my love," he responded

Malana received a phone call and talked for almost thirty minutes. Jamo was getting dress and planning to take her out to dinner. When she got off the phone, she had to return home due to a family emergency and reassured him it was not serious. He wanted to go with her. She reminded him that he needed a passport, an international certificate of vaccination for various shots and a visa in order to stay in her country. "Obtaining these documents will take time, and you can apply for these papers while I am gone, and when I return to D.C., we can leave together for Benin."

Malana was able to get a flight out the next day and asked Jamo to spend the night.

It was Tuesday morning, and Malana was all packed and ready to go. Jamo called a cab; they rode to the airport and arrived two hours before the plane was to leave. They had breakfast at the terminal. As they sat there, she said, "I love you and can't wait to be your wife and to be with you without end."

It was now time for Malana to board the plane. Jamo walked her to the departure gate, gave her an affectionate kiss and said, "I will be waiting for you."

"Farewell," she said and got on the plane.

As the jet took off, he waved and left the airport.

After arriving home, Jamo started to make plans to be with Malana. Late that evening, he went on his computer and received an e-mail from her. She arrived home and would e-mail him soon. He never told his parents or anyone else about her and wanted to wait a little longer before he made the announcement.

For vacation, Jamo's parents made plans to go to St. Kitts. They would be gone for six weeks and asked him to take over the business. This time, he did not mind since it was just a matter of time before he would be gone for good.

Jamo went to work but could not concentrate and was always thinking about Malana. For the next four weeks, he was busy and did not have time to obtain his passport or other vital papers needed for his trip abroad.

He and Malana were e-mailing each other almost every day. She told him there was no rush to make travel plans. She would put together a brokerage account packet and send the information to him in a couple of days. In two months, she was planning to return to D.C.

To make their engagement official, Jamo bought a twenty thousand dollar diamond ring, but her staying with him, in his parents' home, was not possible. He found a one-bedroom apartment in a nice turn of the century building. Since he did not know how long they would be in town, he decided on a month-to-month tenancy; he put down a security deposit and paid six months' rent in advance.

The community where Jamo and his parents lived was like a little village. Everyone knew everybody's business. If a person did not know anything, one was sure to make up something. It did not take long for hearsay to flood the area like a colossal tidal wave.

There were talks that Jamo had a woman in his life, but no one knew who she was. Some saw him going in and out of the hotel with a strange female. She was not from the community. There were even whispers that he was seeing a married woman, because their meetings were so secretive. The talks really heated up when the citizens discovered he had purchased a pricey diamond ring. People were wondering if he bought that ring for her and if so, she was the lucky one.

What the inhabitants did not realize was that this so-called lucky one was a conniving shark that would leave everybody in the community scratching their heads and chewing the fat for months to come.

Jamo's parents had returned from their vacation. They inquired as to how things went while they were away.

"All went well, and sales were extremely good," he said.

His mom and dad were thrilled. They did have a question about the new woman in his life. He asked how they knew. They reminded him that tales travel fast, even to St. Kitts. He could not believe this since he never discussed Malana with anyone.

"She was someone I met on the Internet; she came to D.C. on business for a couple of days and went back home." He assured them it was not serious. They did not press the issue any further. He may have thought his parents fell for that line, but they were not that naïve.

Just as Malana had instructed him to do, Jamo went on the Internet to sign up for an on-line bank account and came up with a unique username and password. He could now transfer money anywhere without having to do it in person. That evening, he e-mailed Malana and informed her as to what he had done.

She e-mailed him back and said, "Excellent. I will see you soon. Take care, my love."

Life was really looking wonderful for Jamo. For the new apartment, he purchased a beautiful bedroom set, a dining room collection and two loveseats; he wanted the place to look like a fortress for his queen but did not want to add too many items; they would only be living there temporarily. When they were ready to depart, they would leave the furnishings behind or have them shipped to Benin.

When Jamo returned to work, he went on-line to check his e-mail. He did not receive any messages from Malana but did receive the following communiqué:

Dear Valued Banking Customer:

It has come to our attention that your bank account information needs updating as part of our continuing commitment to protect your account and to reduce the instances of fraud on our website.

If you could please take ten minutes out of your on-line experience and update your personal records, you will not run into any future problems with the on-line services. Failure to do so will result in suspension of your account.

When you update, your banking session will continue as normal. To bring your bank records up to date, please click on the following link.

Jamo immediately clicked on the link and entered his username and password, followed the instructions and updated his account; he then logged off and continued his work.

The package from Malana had arrived and included prospectus on several brokerage firms and mutual funds. While reading the booklets, he had difficulty deciphering the financial jargon and put the pamphlets aside. He went on-line and thanked her for the information; he would wait for her return to explain the materials to him.

It was now October, and Jamo had not heard from Malana. He went on-line to see if there were any messages from her, but there were none. He needed to know her arrival date, so he could meet her at the airport and take her to their new apartment, but he forgot to ask for her phone number. He did not want her to make hotel reservations and then have to pull out and pay a cancellation fee.

He went to the hotel to see if she had booked a room, but she did not. He sent another e-mail but still heard nothing and was wondering if that call she received was more serious than she had let on. He did not know what to think.

The biggest panic came when Jamo got a statement from the bank, stating that his account was empty. He started to experience palpitations of the heart and knew it was an error on the bank's end.

He rushed to the institution, asked to speak to the manager and implied the bank had made a gross mistake and showed the information to the manger, who said, "It is not a mistake. You transferred all of your money into the World Wide Bank of Benin."

Jamo denied conducting such a transaction; he never came into the bank to perform any business.

The manager informed him that it happened over the Internet.

"Impossible!" Jamo replied. "I would never transfer that much money at one time."

"Nevertheless, someone did," the manager said.

Jamo started to get sick to his stomach, sensed a headache coming and asked, "How could this have happened?" Then he remembered receiving that e-mail from the bank. He hurried back home to retrieve a copy of the message from his computer, returned to the bank and showed the administrator the post.

"The bank never sent that communication," the manager said. "Any correspondence sent to our customers would always include their full name in the salutation and not the words Dear Valued Banking Customer, and the web site would always show a secured key, which would indicate it is a safe server to conduct business." He went to say, "You were the victim of phishing. When you clicked on that link, you virtually gave the cyberspace thieves all the information they needed to get into your account."

Jamo sat there in a stupor and frantically asked, "Who would do such a despicable act, and can the person(s) who did this be arrested and brought to justice, and will I get my money back?"

The manager looked at him with regret and replied, "The answer is no; most of these people operate outside of the United States, and there is nothing the law can do; they have no jurisdiction to go into another country and make arrests, press charges or retrieve your money."

Confused and angry, Jamo wanted to know if there was anyway to tell where the e-mail came from, but the manager could not help him. The bank officer finally told him that the person who stole the money probably left that country. Usually, when someone receives the funds, he or she will close the account and disappear.

To see if there was an e-mail from Malana, Jamo went on-line. There was nothing. He started to worry. Why had she not contacted him? He checked the envelope, which she had sent the materials in, for a return address but there was none. He then remembered the bank that received his money was in Benin. It had finally dawned on him. Malana had stolen his money. *How could I have allowed myself to be taken in by such a person?* Jamo asked himself.

Jamo was so distraught and thought about all the dumb things he did in the name of love, like purchasing a ring, renting an apartment and putting in time and effort into furnishing the place for a woman who did not give a hoop about him. In hindsight, the clues were present: Her haste to come to D.C., her interest in his trust fund, the purported emergency call she received and her persistence to create an on-line bank account.

Love and lust clouded his judgment. He was so good at maneuvering people but could have never seen Malana using him in such a cruel way.

When Jamo was a little boy, he would always hear his grandparents say, "You always get back what you give out."

He thought about those words and wondered was this some kind of reprimand for all the cunning acts he had done in the past, and how was he going to tell his parents. Eventually, they would find out. If they knew about Malana, it would not be long before they would find out about his dilemma. *How do you tell your folks that you lost nearly one million dollars at the click of a mouse?* he pondered.

When Jamo's parents got home, he sat them down and explained what had happened. They were literally in a state of shock. He saw the anger and the disappointment in their faces. What more could he say and how he was sorry for bringing such shame to the family.

Jamo's parents had been optimistic about their son but now wondered if he would ever be ready to take over the business and concluded he had a long way to go before reaching full maturity. They were glad his grandparents were not around to see this awful situation. They would have been saddened.

His parents gave Jamo an ultimatum: He would continue to go to college and still receive a monthly allowance until he was ready to take over the business, or he would be completely on his own with no financial assistance from them. He chose the former.

It was just a matter of time before the rumors started to spread like wild weeds throughout the community. Individuals from all social circles were chitchatting that a beautiful foreign woman ripped off Jamo. Many found it quite amusing that a female would be the one to outfox him and saw it as payback for his treatment of others.

The campus was buzzing with overtones that he was hiding his money to avoid paying taxes.

Some went so far and said, "There was never any trust fund; he made up the whole story to be popular with the women and to be part of the elite inner circle."

Many women on campus did not want to have anything to do with him. Perhaps they were jealous. None of them got his money or that classy diamond ring.

His closest friends were now disassociating themselves from him. He became the abandoned man on campus and the laughing stock of the community. When the money was gone, so were his so-called friends.

Only time will tell if Jamo learned anything from this horrific experience.♦

About the Author

Born in 1946, Vivienne Diane Neal is a storyteller with a wicked sense of humor. Vivienne has been writing articles for over thirty years and started writing fictional short stories in 2007. She gets her story ideas from observing people, places, and things and watching true TV court cases.

Now, semi-retired, she continues to write short stories and articles on love, romance, relationships and other topics of interest.

Sites to Visit:

http://www.oneworldsinglesblog.net

http://lulu.com/spotlight/hmcs1946

http://www.smashwords.com/profile/view/hmcs

http://www.amazon.com/-/e/B003ONO6G4

http://www.amazon.co.uk/-/e/B003ONO6G4

www.ingramcontent.com/pod-product-compliance
Lightning Source LLC
Chambersburg PA
CBHW031103260626
47172CB00001B/192